THE LIAR & THE KNIGHT

REECE A. CAVEN

ACKNOWLEDGEMENTS

This book is dedicated to my 6th Grade teacher Mrs. Lucas, who read my zombie story to the class and told them why she liked it. Mrs. Lucas, teachers like you are why people grow up to chase their dreams. Thank you.

I ALSO WANT to credit my editor Jason Letts and my cover artist Leon Ning.

PROLOGUE

A bead of sweat dove and crashed onto parchment, blotting a line of fresh ink. The parchment shook and made slight squiggles in the lines as the quill sliced by. It was a hot day, and a fire crackled in the hearth. Against the walls were shelves of dishes and books, small ornaments, and a few large vases with neglected Cantha Leaf, their white flowers wilted and their thick green stems drooping from their lack of care.

There was a spiral staircase to one side of the room, leading up to the second floor, and on the far wall, there was the open entrance to the kitchen. In between were a few stiff wooden chairs as a poor excuse for furniture, a large red rug half covered by heaps of cluttered scrolls and parchments strewn across the floor, and a man, curly-headed with a high-collared, embroidered yellow tunic and bronze-colored skin, hunched over a table, frantically drawing on this parchment.

"Yevnir Goldleaf!" A muffled shout rang through the almost empty house, startling the man at work. It was a woman's voice, thick with an accent. He hurried his drawing, his wrist weak and his lines flawed.

"Where is it, Goldleaf?" she yelled from just outside his door.

The man swallowed the lump in his throat as he glanced nervously at the door. He flung the parchment out of his way and it drifted to the ground. On its face, a crude drawing of a squirrel-like figure with stripes across its body holding a circular disk in its paws. This was not meant for the fire.

He pulled a gold coin from his pocket and twiddled it with his fingers before tucking it back into his pocket. The hearth blazed and spit embers, and when the large figures outside blocked out the sunshine from the windows, the fire became his only light.

He stumbled toward it, wading through parchments and scrolls and almost tripping on a leather-bound book hidden amidst the mess. Before the hearth, he dropped to his knees and started ripping crumpled parchments from where they were tucked under his arm. Every other second, he glanced at the door, expecting it to burst open, wondering in terror if that little iron lock would hold. As he tossed his documents into the fire, he reveled at how they soaked up the orange light and shriveled to nothingness like decaying fruit.

Another knock.

"He home now." This voice was different from the first, deeper and slightly quieter—a man.

"No! Master Yevnir is not home!" shouted the man inside—the artist—Yevnir. "He is at the port conducting business."

"Then we wait for him," the woman said. "Open your door, maid."

The artist paused, still on his knees. A slight smirk formed at the corner of his lips and his trembling hands gradually calmed to stillness. "I am a servant!" he said. "Not a maid."

"What is difference?" the deep voice answered.

"Well," the artist started, his head tilting to the side, "I guess you could say—"

"Open the door, servant!" shouted the woman.

The artist stood and went to the door, unbolting the lock and opening it. A short-haired, dark-skinned woman with a golden necklace stared straight at him, and a large, pot-bellied, and broad-shouldered brute stared down at him with a toothy smile.

"If you are going to come in for tea," said the artist, "we should introduce ourselves. My name is Harold Bremington," he lied. The brute smothered his words with an open palm, squeezing his cheeks before pushing his head into the wall and holding him there. The artist felt as though this brute's hand would explode his head like a watermelon.

"Tea," chuckled the brute. "Tea."

"Start searching, Jakka," said the woman, and the brute released him.

Bent over, gasping for the air the giant palm had denied him, the artist reached out an arm in desperation. "Please do not make a mess! Master Yevnir will kill me. I still have not finished sorting his papers."

"Go, servant."

The suggestion shocked him, but he wasn't one to question an opportunity for self-preservation. "As you wish, ma'am." He got up and rushed out of the door as the two intruders tossed the house.

Outside, surrounded by pine trees that littered the ground with orange needles like he had littered his own floor with parchment, he ran. A smile grew on his face until he was laughing. His legs moved hastily beneath him, with a sort of skip every once in a while, and his arms moved awkwardly, as if he weren't quite sure how running worked. It wasn't until he turned a corner and started down the mountainside that he finally slowed to a walk.

The artist came to a thickly wooded ridge where the slope flattened slightly. "Damn pirates," he said aloud, chuckling to himself as his chest rose and fell. Shaking his head, he reached a hand down into his pocket to fetch the coin. He rolled it over his fingers and tossed it in the air, caught it, and slid it gracefully back into his pocket.

A goat trail weaved around the hard part of the descent, and he followed it for a while until it intersected with a dirt road, then he followed that. An old man and his donkey, with a cart hitched to its back, walked toward him on the road. The man had gray hair and he labored over each step. The donkey seemed to keep pace with him out of respect. “Silas save ya,” said the old man in passing.

“And you, friend.” The artist smiled at the brief interaction, then stopped in his tracks, the elder behind him now. “How much for the cart?” He turned toward the old man and his donkey.

The elder looked surprised. “Don’t you wanna know what’s in it?”

“Not particularly, no. How much? For the donkey too.”

“I can’t part with old Selly for much less than a fortune, but I’ll give you what I got in this cart for 10 silver. You trade in Edran coin, I’ll give it ya for nine.”

“How about a Gramon gold?” the artist tossed his coin to the old man, who caught it sprightly, his eyes widening.

“I can’t take this much. No, no. This much is trouble for someone like me. Please, take it back.”

“I won’t,” said the artist, “and on second thought, keep the cart, and your donkey too. Have a good day, friend.”

“Well, thank you!” exclaimed the old man, “I can’t believe it! Now you won’t go destitute on my behalf, would ya? I’d hate for me to take all you got.”

The artist laughed heartily. “There is plenty more where that came from. Enjoy it. It’s a beautiful day.” He turned the other way with a smile on his face, thinking if those pirates happened to run into the old man, they might find the gold and it would buy him some more time. Gramon golds weren't easy to come by on the island. The pirates would stop to question him, and he would send them the wrong way.

Whistling an upbeat tune, he was content with himself and the warm sun that peeked through the branches and touched his cheeks. He cut off the dirt road to a more ancient trail, hidden to most, revealed to few, and it led him to a small pond fed by a waterfall. Purple wildflowers spattered the tall grass, and the sound of rushing water filled his ears. He walked over an old stone bridge, covered in moss so that it was more green than gray, and lay down in the grass and wildflowers on the other side. His feet ached from all the walking, and he needed a rest.

If there weren't a crew of pirates looking for him, he may have fallen asleep right there, with the sound of water splashing and flowing as it fell, the sun beating down on him, and the tall grass like feather pillows beneath his back.

"Goldleaf. You should not sleep." This was a woman's voice, thickly accented, and playful as if she were in on some joke he was not privy to.

He struggled to his feet. "Goldleaf? Are you talking about Master Yevnir? I am just his servant." He always thought it best to stay consistent with his lies.

"I know you. Who you are. What you took from me." The voice seemed to be coming from somewhere else now, the rushing water throwing off the noise. He looked around and saw a figure darting between two trees, and he ran scared in the other direction.

"You will give it to me!" the woman shouted angrily.

He turned quickly toward a thick pine. A flash of an elbow crashed into his face, and he fell stiffly into the pine needles. His vision was blurry. His head rang. His cheek burned with pain where the sharp elbow had connected. From his back, he saw the pointed tips of pine trees like a row of javelins flying toward the clouds. A large yellow bird flew through the blue sky, and he followed its path before something stepped in to block his view. It was one of the pirates, then it was two, and then it was six, surrounding him, looking down at him with ivory masks.

CHAPTER ONE

"Storms don't hit these waters unless there's somethin' to follow."

Sir Willam clutched tight to the portside rail of the ship. Somewhere out in the dark turbulent waters of the Callaseen Ocean, he put his faith in this deckhand, a tower of a man, with three fingers to each hand and as many teeth in his mouth. They stood near each other—near enough, at least, for the knight to smell his body odor. The scent was like rotten eggs dropped into a bowl of curdled milk.

That was the general smell on the *Loyal Blue*, this merchant ship from the ports of Woodsworth. It was quite large for a cog, with a high-reaching mast and a sail boasting the royal sigil of house Antaeus of Edra, and it was run by a mere fifteen crewmen, besides the captain and first mate. Most of the crew aboard the *Loyal Blue* were as tough as they were odorous, though this deckhand, Raf, was an overachiever among his peers and had a singularly pungent stench.

Sir Willam had spent most of his week on ship above deck, preferring the smell of the ocean to the mingling of armpits in the hull. So, when Raf had come to stand near him, he'd almost felt as though there was no escape.

A shout came from above. "Somethin' out there." This was a boy's voice. Sir Willam tilted his head up to see a rascally, wiry youth up in the crow's nest. "Go on, Sir," he said, looking down with cheery eyes, "give it a good look."

The boy, Tren, had the same features and unwavering enthusiasm as Sir Willam's younger brother, Sampson. The only discernible differences were the scars across his cheek, the long hair he had tied up in a ponytail, and his obsession with the game of chivin, through which he had already robbed the knight of four Gramon silvers.

"Will you come down when the storm catches us?" Sir Willam asked him.

"Aye, Sir, I'll be right down to show you what's what."

"He don't know what's what!" Raf cackled. "None of them do."

Sir Willam looked back up at the boy and watched him excitedly peer through his telescope.

"This is amazing, Sir!" Tren shouted down. "It never storms in the Callaseen Strait."

That's what the knight had been led to believe. Now it seemed there was an exception: *Unless there's somethin' to follow.* Sir Willam suddenly noticed Raf smiling and watched him intently as he drifted away from the rail, an oddly giddy bounce in his step. With a determined squint, the knight looked over the water to find whatever "something" lurked beneath the violent tide. He saw nothing, just the luminous black and gray clouds of a quickly approaching storm. The rumble of thunder was more of a crumple from so far, like someone was crinkling leaves from a hiding place below deck.

He'd never been out at sea when a storm hit. In fact, he'd barely been out at sea at all. He watched the clouds roll in with the dread of a mischievous child waiting for a beating, although he couldn't help but be sucked in by the allure of it all. The way the clouds rolled over each other, running and colliding, and how, when lightning shot through them, they revealed themselves to be not these dark, scary things, but only shadowed versions of those beautiful puffs of white you see on a bright sunny day.

Behind him, the crew actively braced for the storm's coming. The first mate, Savvin, a short, dark-skinned man with a limp, came down the stairs of the quarterdeck shouting orders; four crewmen do this, six crewmen that, tie this off, push those barrels tight. All the while, Sir Willam watched from the rail.

The crewmen took up a shanty as they worked. It was a deep-voiced, ominous melody about ships sinking and being split in two by the will of a storm. Yet, at the end of every verse, there was a crescendo of morbid laughter as the crew shouted, "To your ship and to you, but not to the *Loyal Blue*!"

It didn't take long before the rain started dripping and then pouring. He curiously observed the jolt and sway of the tide, even when the rain was pelting his face and drenching his cloak. The switch from gentle waves to rough waters came too gradually to track, but once it was there, the ship fought and struggled with its carrier rather than gliding harmoniously above it. Still, the knight searched the waters with his eyes.

"See it yet?" The boy was next to him now with the same resolute cheer despite the rain.

"I haven't seen a thing," Sir Willam said. He looked from the boy's soaked tan shirt back to the water.

Between the harsh rain and the way the tide bobbled the ship back and forth, looking alone brought on a headache. He cursed himself for accepting this quest. While on his way home from his last job, breaking up a brief scuffle between a landlord and their tenant near Effington, he'd seen a courier galloping toward him on the cobbled road.

He'd recognized the man as soon as he saw him, bouncing in his saddle, and his first reaction was to pull his reins and press his boots into his old horse's side to turn him in the other direction. He was so close to Horntree, his home; so close to bliss, and his brothers; so close to fishing, late nights singing and drinking with his oldest friends, and to settling down by a cozy fire to get the rest that had evaded him for so many years.

Sir Willam had slapped his reins hard and pushed his horse to the brink of exhaustion avoiding this courier. He did not intend to let him delay his return to Horntree any longer. This was the same man who'd delivered him the news of his last quest, and that awful one with the Sceuorg that had brought him so much fame. The message he'd carried was of no interest to the knight, and so he tried to run from it before that detestable thing called honor could force him to answer whatever call to duty it contained.

His horse was tired though, old Baron, and so the courier caught him quickly, and asked, "Why do you flee from me, Sir?" to which the knight had replied, "Just give me the damn message." The courier had handed him a letter enclosed with golden wax and stamped with a familiar holly leaf seal. Sir Willam didn't know whether to smile, thinking of his old friend Yevnir and all the adventures they'd once had in Bordae, or to throw the letter to the ground and circle Baron about so that his hooves stomped the wretched thing into the dirt.

So, he found himself on a ship in the middle of the Callaseen Strait, sailing to an island he had never been to, because he had an overworked old horse that couldn't outrun a courier, and because he was too loyal a friend.

His squinting and searching in the rolling tide was beginning to feel pointless. Savvin had pulled Tren from the deck to do some job in the hull, leaving Sir Willam still searching in vain for that mysterious something. His headache was coming on strong now. That is, before he saw the blue fish. After that, the creeping pain behind his eyes seemed to dissipate and be replaced with an openness that only wonder could fill. His eyes widened and focused. He held his breath.

They were the shiniest blips of light he had seen in the ocean, whipping through the water, dipping and diving deeper without ever breaking the surface. He could see brief glimpses of their light from afar, and as they started to come closer to the ship, he leaned over the rail to meet them.

They turned and started coming straight toward the ship. He could see their light flickering and glimmering as it came toward him as if the sun were out and shining and they were catching its rays.

"I'm ready." Sir Willam thought this was his voice at first until he looked over and saw Raf back at the rail. His eyes were closed and his head tilted toward the sky, another creature embracing the sun as if it weren't hiding behind storm clouds. *That deckhand seems to lose things a lot. His teeth, his fingers, and now his mind. He's been a seaman too long.*

A couple of fish had reached the ship now and were circling in wide arcs. The knight leaned over farther to make out their features. The fisherman in him felt a nagging desire to reach in and grab them. He wanted to hold them and feel their shining scales, to have them at the end of his line and know if they fought like bass or resigned themselves like carp.

These were saltwater fish, though, creatures that lived in the deep, whereas he had only ever held the slimy, bottom-feeding fish of the shallow ponds and smooth-flowing streams he'd grown up around. He started to realize he was out of his depth the closer they got. His mind went to what kind of hook he'd need. What bait would these blue fish take? Then, he started to wonder if they were fish at all.

He saw what he thought was an arm. No, it couldn't have been. He saw fins swirling around what looked like a head.

"I'm ready," Raf repeated. The sky lit up from a piercing bolt of lightning and the crew's shanty-singing and stomping around the deck was muffled to incoherence by a deafening crack of thunder. As soon as the sky ceased its shaking, the noise was replaced by an odd hum that glided on the waves.

Sir Willam saw another flash of blue below. *Seven now.* Tilting his head curiously, he looked up at Raf as the sound faded. "Ready for wha—"

A wave crashed over the rail and the ship tilted violently, sending them scrambling and fumbling for purchase. The knight lost his footing and landed on his stomach. As he slid, he desperately grabbed hold of a rope connected to the mast. The ship slapped down on the water and the wave passed, and he was catapulted right back to the portside rail, sliding on his belly into a barrel.

When he rolled to his back and looked up, his feet touching the wood bulwarks, he was staring into the cold blue eyes of a devilish dark-gray creature. Its giant blue pupils seemed to shake as thunder cracked in the distance, and he recognized the blue shine for what it was. They were never fish.

Its ears were long and droopy like a donkey's, the only unscaled part of its body. The red gills that sat under its wide-set jaw and ran halfway down its slender neck started to vibrate as it opened its mouth to continue that soft hum he'd heard just moments ago. Its body shined with a sort of grayish-blue hue, and its scales were glossy with slime. Its feet were webbed and there were spiky fins on the outside of its forearms with tentacle-like suction cups on the inside. Something about the sound, and the creature itself, was beautiful in its own, terrible way, like how a bear can be beautiful and still rip you to pieces.

The knight was too enamored, even when it revealed its jagged fangs, to recognize it as a threat.

"Sir?" It was Tren's voice, quiet and curious. The knight looked over to where Raf had been standing just before the wave hit, and saw the young crewman, wrapped in the scaled arms of the same sort of creature that loomed above Sir Willam on the rail. It was on Tren's back, suctioned to him like a giant octopus. The humming intensified and became even more abrasive, to the point where Sir Willam almost covered his ears.

Tren looked completely at peace. "Stay still," said the knight. He reached slowly for his dagger, keeping the curious creature above him in his peripheral as it sized him up, tilting its head from side to side and bellowing its oddly seductive hum.

He was sure the rest of the crew must have been in a frenzy as this happened, but he was so frozen in this stalemate, in the game of trying not to move too fast and provoke these creatures, that all he could focus on was Tren and the two monsters. Tren was just a few steps away yet unreachable.

"Do you hear that, Sir?" Tren said. His cheerfulness had dissolved into something more substantial. He wasn't happy anymore, nor was he excited or jubilant. He was at peace, complete peace, while the storm raged and the waves crashed. While the crew fumbled for organization, the ship was being boarded by creatures from the depths.

The thing tightened its grip around Tren. "It's singing to me, just like mum used to," the boy said. "She wants me to come home."

Sir Willam was shocked at how he could be so calm and so much like his little brother that even though he had known this boy for less than a week, he felt that whatever this creature might do to him he'd rather it be done to himself. His dagger was almost fully out of its sheath, and he watched the creature's shiny blue eyes to try to find a tell, to try to figure out if it meant Tren harm.

A crack of thunder boomed, and Sir Willam yanked his dagger from its sheath. The beast flung itself backward over the rail with Tren wrapped tightly in its arms. Sir Willam threw his dagger, but it was too late. It barely missed the beast as it pulled Tren into the water with it. "Tren!"

His dagger embedded itself into the woodwork of the stairs. He pounded his fist against the floorboard and screamed for the boy. He screamed, not just for Tren but for Sampson, because in the moment there was no difference.

"Don't let 'em take you over!" This was Captain Tarrick's voice, and it shook Sir Willam into action. It seemed to shake the creature above him too. Its hum dissipated into a sort of howl, and it hopped off the railing only to meet the knight's boot halfway down. His kick sent it sprawling over the side, and he jumped to his feet.

It was this exact moment that Sir Willam felt naked. He'd left his armor and his horse with an old blacksmith friend in Woodsworth. His armor had been in desperate need of repair since his fight with the Sceuorg, but he would've still preferred to fight with his armor bent and broken than without it.

"Over here!" One of the creatures had Savvin wrapped in its slender arms. Its fangs ripped at the loose flesh on the back of his arm. Sir Willam moved but the deckhand got there first.

Another creature leaped at them from the quarterdeck above. In one motion the knight yanked his sword from its scabbard and slashed straight through the creature's midsection. It landed in two pieces with a wet thud, and the blood that splattered Sir Willam's face was indistinguishable from the rain.

Raf had made quick work of the creature feasting on the first mate, and the poor man lay moaning and clutching at his brutalized triceps. The crew gathered quickly on the main deck, wielding knives, axes, and short swords. Captain Tarrick fell in beside Sir Willam, all of them on their toes and with their eyes on a swivel as the rain continued to pelt their skin.

"What are they?" yelled the knight. An arc of lightning flashed in the distance, breaking the surface of the dark-gray sky. Two more creatures appeared at the quarterdeck, slithering toward them with an awful ticking sound.

Somewhere in the water, a third creature shrieked desperately as if it were drowning. It howled like a mother cradling the cool corpse of her infant. It gasped and bellowed like it was trying to swallow the ocean and bring the ship down with it.

Sir Willam tasted iron and salt on his tongue and knew it was the blood of the creature he had killed. The blood of what? He had never seen anything like it. He had no name to describe his enemy, these monsters that had taken a young boy from his future.

Anger boiled in his chest and rose to his throat. "Captain!" he shouted.

Captain Tarrick was shivering, from the cold or from the fear, Sir Willam couldn't tell, but he watched the creatures on the deck with wide eyes that didn't move as he said, "Sirens."

Another siren ticked its song from atop the figurehead at the bow of the ship. Sir Willam saw the crew start to break. They shuffled toward the rails and away from the mast in the middle of the deck. Another shrill gasp sounded from the ocean.

"Stay tight!" the knight shouted.

A deckhand broke off and made a bolt for the captain's cabin. The sirens descended on him before he could reach the door, but the knight was close behind, yelling, "Stay together! I got these two."

The deckhand was on his back with the two sirens hovering over him. They punched down violently and screamed some sort of guttural battle cry with their tongues flying from their mouths and their ears flailing around their heads.

Sir Willam shoved one into the cabin door so hard it broke the hinges and fell straight through. He turned to stab the other, but it smothered him before he could thrust his sword. Landing on his back with the thing on top of him, he flailed and arched his hips to no avail. It grabbed his head in its slimy hands and banged it against the floor planks. A scream rattled from its mouth, engulfing him in the awful smell of rotten fish.

He tried in vain to break its suctioned grip. His head smashed against the wood. A sharp pain ran through his body as he fumbled at his belt for his dagger. His head hit again. The pain throbbed in his skull.

A unified scream filled the air, and the siren flew off him, followed by three yelling crewmen who carried it with its webbed feet dragging and pinned it against the wall. Before it could react, it was surrounded, and the crewmen were stabbing it relentlessly. It stood, taking their attacks, until finally, it crumpled onto the damp wood with its shiny blue eyes still staring straight.

Sir Willam heard the smashing of glass inside the captain's cabin.

Another siren lay dead beside him with an axe buried in its skull, and Raf had one three-fingered hand pressing another siren's head into the floor planks as he sawed its ears off with a knife. Still lying on his back, the knight felt a presence loom over him and looked over to see Captain Tarrick reaching his hand down.

He took it and let the captain pull him up. His head spun as he shakily stood and brushed the slime off his cloak.

Balance had not quite returned to him when he heard another loud crash of glass smashing and saw the sirens crawling through the captain's broken windows. The first thing he did was bend down and pick up his sword, then, stepping over the flattened cabin door, he raised it in both hands.

Three of them postured toward him, moving in front of Captain Tarrick's bed. They whipped their tongues out and flopped their grey, donkey-like ears around their heads. Sir Willam saw a fourth behind them, climbing past the windows to the quarterdeck above.

A stream of crewmen came rushing into the cabin behind him. There were eight seamen and one knight packed into the room, staring with violent intent at the three invading sirens. The creatures bent like coils ready to spring and Sir Willam tightened his grip on his sword.

"Captain Tarrick," the knight said firmly.

"Yes, Sir?"

The sirens started a wild cacophony of ticking, their heads jerking stiffly, and their noises started to mingle until they synchronized. Sir Willam wondered with fury how that same song had enticed Tren into accepting the siren's slimy embrace.

"Raf," the knight said.

"Aye, Sir?"

"Through the middle with me. The rest of you stick to the walls and flank. Ready?"

The sirens seemed hesitant—no, patient. *What are they doing?* All three of their heads shot upward and they were blinking in unison. Two young crewmen stepped forward, both just a few years older than Tren.

"Not yet!" Sir Willam shouted at them. They didn't hear, or they didn't listen, but regardless, they continued forward, slack-jawed and limp-armed. Their weapons clattered to the ground.

"Get yer arses back here!" the captain pleaded.

Sir Willam looked around quickly and then made his decision. "Charge!" he yelled.

The crew spurred into action behind him, and he bowled straight through the middle of the two crewmen in front. Splitting them apart, he jumped at the sirens with his sword rising above his head.

With a downward strike, his sword lodged itself halfway through the sheen and slimy shoulder of the middle siren. The crew and the sirens collided violently around the knight, and the sirens lashed out twice as viciously as the ones on the deck. Sir Willam jostled with his sword, trying to yank the blade out, but the siren walked forward, unwavering in its shrieking and ticking.

To his left, a siren flung Captain Tarrick into his own desk, smashing the wood and sending scrolls and maps up into the air. Sir Willam glanced from the siren in front of him to where Captain Tarrick lay splayed out on the floorboards. Two crewmen slashed at the siren approaching their captain, but the wounds weren't deep enough, and the siren just swatted them away the same way it had Captain Tarrick.

Sir Willam's siren clutched the steel of his sword and pulled itself toward the hilt with all its effort, inching itself forward on his blade. Captain Tarrick's siren stood over him, stopped in place. To his right, the other crewmen wrestled with the third siren, but he couldn't keep track of their progress.

Captain Tarrick's siren bent down and grabbed him with one hand on his neck and the other clawing into his belly. Sir Willam turned and looked into the blue eyes of the siren stuck to his sword. It wanted him to fear those eyes, but fear had left him long ago. He made one more desperate yank. The siren reached for him with both arms. He glanced at Captain Tarrick and then twisted his sword with all his might.

At the same time Sir Willam felt his own siren touch him with the tips of its claws, he heard Captain Tarrick let out an agonizing scream. With his blade now horizontal he slapped one of the claws of his own siren away and stepped around to grab it by its ear.

"Help me!" the captain cried.

With a fist full of siren ear and his other hand wrapped tight around his sword handle, Sir Willam yanked down to get the siren off its balance and then rushed forward, colliding with the other siren. His blade sliced the back of its neck as it dug into Captain Tarrick with its claws.

Sir Willam tried to keep moving forward but his momentum was gone. The blade was stuck in one siren's neck and above the other's ribs, gluing them together. The captain fell to the floor and rolled out of the way as the sirens flailed around and pushed on each other.

For a brief moment, Sir Willam stayed in this fight with them.

He head-butted one and punched the other, and as he ducked and threw a wild overhand, he lost his grip on his sword. His fist connected with a wet jaw and the two sirens fell backward together, leaving Sir Willam standing upright watching them flail like turtles stuck on their backs.

The whole group of crewmen, including two fresh ones from the deck, swarmed the two sirens and stomped and stabbed them to death. Sir Willam looked at Captain Tarrick, writhing and groaning on the floor. Claw marks bloodied his stomach, but they hadn't gone deep enough to cause any real damage.

The knight offered him his hand and pulled him up. "We must move, Captain. No time for pain."

Sir Willam rushed to his sword and pushed with a boot on the dead sirens, pulling aggressively with both hands until it came free. With the three sirens killed and his sword in hand, the knight led the crew out of the cabin, excluding Raf, who stayed behind collecting his trophies.

The sky still spat its harsh rain as Sir Willam stepped over the downed cabin door with a squelch in his boots. As he made his way to the mast, the whole crew gathered on the main deck, one young spotter missing. That's when Sir Willam remembered the fourth siren on the quarterdeck.

Around the main mast, the crew stood defensively, panting and rocking with anticipation. The knight joined them. "What happened to the other siren?" he asked.

"It ran scared!" said one of the crewmen.

"There won't be another." They all turned to see Raf coming

out of the cabin, standing over a siren's corpse and holding a handful of floppy gray ears.

"How in Eben's green earth do you know that?" Savvin asked, clutching his bleeding triceps.

"'Cause I know." Raf pulled a long necklace from inside his shirt, and instead of a pendant, an old shriveled-up siren's ear dangled from the end of it.

They stayed huddled around the mast for an hour, hearing faint cries from the ocean. Sir Willam imagined that last siren, somewhere in the deep, slowly swallowing Tren the way a snake swallows a rabbit. Was the one who got away the same one who took Tren? He had no way of knowing. Maybe it had devoured Tren quickly and come back aboard the *Loyal Blue* for its second course, or maybe that siren never came up again. Either way, the thought fueled his steady rocking, the racing in his mind, and the tight grip he kept around the hilt of his sword.

Every once in a while, they would hear what they thought was a crew member screaming for help. At every crack of thunder, they jumped to attention and clutched their weapons. Once, after a long, chilling sound that seemed to dissipate as a wave crashed into the ship, Sir Willam bewilderedly said, "I thought sirens were supposed to have beautiful voices, enough to lure you in. Sounds like a cow dying to me."

Most of the crew were silent, but Raf, wearing his ear trophies proudly over his shirt and staring out into the dark waters, said, "You probably thought they were supposed to be pretty women, lying on rocks naked as a newborn too."

Sir Willam nodded.

"Paritine sirens ain't the same as the ones you heard about, sir. They're more scary lookin' here, aye, but don't be fooled 'cause a beast looks tougher. It's the pretty ones that carry the poison."

The storm settled after a while, and the clouds gave way like curtains to the sun's rays. The whole crew, soaked, shivering, and somber from the death of their young spotter, seemed to bask in the light. For a while, nobody moved, except to bounce and shiver as the sun dried their wet clothes. Until Captain Tarrick had finally had enough.

The captain scanned the water, then inched his way to the rail and hesitantly peeked over the sides.

"Back to it, lads!" he shouted, skipping into motion.

He began climbing the stairs to the quarterdeck, back to his position at the wheel, and Sir Willam meant to follow him, but he saw the deckhand walk by and succumbed to a sudden urge to grab his arm. "Raf."

"Sir?"

"Why don't their songs work?"

Raf had tensed at Sir Willam's touch, but now he settled into an unsettling look of complete comfort. "They worked well enough earlier," Raf said. "The young lads, remember?"

The knight tilted his head, thinking about how the young crewmen had dropped their weapons and walked toward the sirens in the cabin, and how easily Tren had resigned himself to his own death. "Why them?"

Raf shrugged. "You mean, why not us?" He grinned deviously and patted Sir Willam hard on the shoulder before making his way back toward the dead sirens in the cabin.

The knight turned his attention back to Captain Tarrick, who had just finished climbing the stairs. He went after him, wiggling his dagger free from the wood of one of the lower stairs before climbing them.

Up on the quarterdeck, the breeze hit Sir Willam harder, and he caught a great whiff of ocean air, fresh and salty, while his brown hair blew across his face and his black cloak flapped at his sides.

"Are you going to be alright, Captain?" Sir Willam stood leaning on the rail while the captain reset his course, his dagger sheathed and the tip of his sword pressed into a floorboard beside his foot.

"I'll be fine." Captain Tarrick held his stomach with one hand as he settled his other one on the wheel. "The boy won't be."

"We have to go after the last siren," the knight said.

Captain Tarrick chuckled nervously. "And what? Dive in after him? Tren is gone, Sir, and you have a quest to complete, don't you? There's no getting him back."

"There's setting things right."

"Didn't you tell me you liked to fish?" The captain's voice was shaky.

Sir Willam didn't respond.

The captain looked away from him. "Don't you think the fish wish they could jump out of the water and kill you for taking their brothers and sisters?"

The knight sighed and shook his head. He thought of ways he could find that siren and put his sword through it, then he thought about his friend Yevnir waiting for him in Pastora, someone whom he could still save rather than avenge. "How often do ships get attacked on this route?" he asked, stepping closer to the wheel.

"Been captain of this ship for ten long years, Sir, and this is me– me first encounter with 'em."

"What about—"

"Raf? He worked on the *Wayfinder* before. Exploratory vessel. Don't you worry about this happenin' again. You'll be safe on the way back. Lightning don't strike the same ship twice, although it'll be a different ship that you'll board." The captain's hands trembled at the wheel.

Sir Willam's were rock steady.

"Oh, look!" Captain Tarrick pointed to the sky, his other hand shielding his eyes from the sun. Sir Willam saw, soaring gracefully overhead, a group of four large birds. They were as big as swans, but instead of black or white, they were a bright golden yellow, with black-tipped feathers and long eagle-like talons.

"I've never seen anything like them," the knight said, standing there in awe as they passed. It was the second time he'd been left dumbfounded in only a few hours. This time, with his adrenaline finally settling, he could enjoy it. He thought about the seagulls on the east coast of Edra and the way they would cover the beaches in the early morning.

"What are they called?" he asked.

"Huh?" The captain seemed distant, as if between seeing the birds and hearing Willam's voice he'd had a whole conversation that the knight hadn't been a part of.

"The birds."

"Oh, those are torpins," said the captain. He smiled uneasily. "I felt the same when I first saw 'em. Breathtakin' creatures, aren't they?"

"Does seeing them mean we're close?"

"It don't mean we're close necessarily. Torpins nest in Pastora, but they can fly forever. I saw one near Boncopa once."

"That far south?" asked the knight.

Captain Tarrick smiled. "I see yer face, but I promise ya, I'm too much a fool to lie outright and too honest to embellish."

Sir Willam finally felt safe enough to sheathe his sword. It was already wiped clean by the rain, but he gave it an extra wipe with his cloak for good measure before sliding it into the scabbard at his belt. "How will we know when we're close?"

The captain was calmer now too. There were monsters in the deep, but the skies had given him comfort. His eyes were closed, and Sir Willam could see his lips moving, just quivering slightly to accompany the words he said in his mind. *He's praying to Silas*, Sir Willam thought, *as if it weren't us who killed the sirens.*

"You know, you can get lost out here, Sir Willam," Captain

Tarrick said. "On the water, I mean. On the island too. And it wouldn't even be too bad a thing." He opened his eyes with another uneasy smile, but this time his face seemed to relax and the ease came back to him.

He remembered that feeling the captain spoke of, but it was so old a memory that he couldn't grasp it as it floated by on the breeze.

"So," said the knight, "how will we know?"

The captain turned to him, and although he was still shaky, in pain, and in fear of his life, there was joy in his voice when he said, "You'll see green."

CHAPTER TWO

Green meant land.

The green of grass rolling up the hills, the green of lily pads that carpeted an eastern shore, and even the green of algae clinging to the jagged coastal rocks. Then the breeze brushed his cheek, carrying a cool mist, and in that moment he smiled —the kind of closed-eyed smile one made after sinking their teeth into a savory cut of meat or a sweet apple pastry.

The merchant's ship lulled and bobbed under his feet as they sailed into calmer waters, so that a smile like this could be enjoyed and not thrown off-balance by aggressive waves. When he was ready to open his eyes, he did so to the discovery of a new color on the horizon. He saw the pale brown of stiff wooden docks on the port ahead, stretching out into the bay like the fingers of a giant hand.

"Here she is. Get ready to dock!" yelled the ship's captain. "Will you be wantin' a guide, Sir?" he asked, climbing down the stairs from the quarterdeck. "Pastora ain't big, but she'll suck you in if you let 'er."

Sir Willam took his hands from the taffrail and turned to face the captain. His black cloak rose and waved in the coastal wind, hanging on by the tree-shaped bronze brooch at his collar. “No, thank you, Captain. I can find my own way, and if not, I’ll be just as happy to get lost.”

Captain Tarrick gave him a nod then did a double take. “It surely ain’t my business what knights get up to, but didn’t you say this trip was urgent?”

“Important, not urgent. It’s quite a different thing. The person I’m here for loves his theatrics. Those can wait, as far as I’m concerned. I’d like to see this island a bit first.”

“Aye, Sir.” The captain shrugged and went back to his place at the wheel, and soon the crew was tying the vessel to the docks. When the ship was tied off, the crew got to work unloading it. They hurried back and forth with heavy loads of barrels and sacks, each man carrying his fill at every trip.

Sir Willam watched as the crew furled the sail displaying the Edran banner. It was a big square of light-blue cloth and in its center, the sigil of house Antaeus, the royal family of Edra, was in black. Their sigil was a giant reaching for a star, and at its feet was the vague outline of a forest for scale. The blue sail rippled with the wind as the crewmen furled it closed. The knight smirked at this last confirmation that he was far from home and then took his proper leave of everybody.

First, he sought out the merchant who owned the ship. He said his thanks and shook his hand tenderly, then found the captain and shook his hand fondly, and the crewmen’s hands firmly. All of them wished him good luck on his adventures, although none of them, including himself, knew what those might be.

Stepping onto the dock, the knight rummaged through his satchel to find the letter he’d received a few weeks prior—the reason he had crossed the sea. He pulled the crumpled parchment out and tried to shake it dry, then flattened it the best he could. The corners were stained with drops of red wax and little blots of what looked like blood, now slightly smeared from the rain. He read it.

To Sir Willam Hornsby,

Will, my dearest friend. I have no one else to turn to. I'm afraid my schemes will soon catch up with me, as you always said they would. If only I had stayed in Bordae. How I miss my Edran roads, the canals in the city, and my Bordaen wines! How I miss the vineyards and the late nights in Groll's tavern. You remember the ones. Sweet, slender beauties at my arm and big, hefty dames at yours. I miss the safety of the city gates and the danger of a midnight gamble!

I know you would feel the same if ever you left the continent. That is not to say that you wouldn't find a love for this land though, as I have. Pastora is a sort of paradise to me. It is a land of magic, old friend. I have seen things here that even you would shudder to stand against, and things so stunning that I could stare at them for weeks on end. You will truly love it if you come, and you must come.

You see, I am in a bit of a jam here on the island. One I cannot free myself of alone. I need your help. That is all I can say on the matter. You will know why if you make the journey. If by chance you get this letter, meet me at the Hollow Mountain Inn in the port town of Biverna. Find a merchant ship in Woodsworth. Any will do. I will know of your arrival before you reach the inn.

Please, Will, answer my call. I know I have been a hindrance to you, over the many years of our friendship, but I would not ask if I weren't in dire need and in perilous danger. It is not a rumor that there is luck aplenty on this green island, but all luck must run out, just as every sunny day must end in darkness. If you don't come to Pastora, I am afraid I won't ever see the dawn again.

Your friend,
Yevnir Goldleaf

Sir Willam shook his head, folded the letter into his pocket, and thought, *You really do have a knack for drama, Yev.* Looking up at the town of Biverna, the knight wondered what mischief his old friend had stirred up this time. From his view on the dock, the land still held its green hue, only spotted with the browns and tans of wood.

The structures in Biverna were almost all made of wood, save for a few stone houses that looked like they had been fetched straight from the sea. The stones of these houses were dark and smooth, as if they were always wet, and moss grew so thick from some that they looked like a grassy hill when looking at them straight on. But all of these structures, wood and stone, had roofs layered with dirt from which grass grew, making them look like they had risen up from the ground.

This architectural custom baffled the knight, who was used to the thatched roofs of the Edran villages back home or the tiled ones in the cities. Yet, noticing a house that grew dandelions and sprouts of dangly dark flowers from its roof, he wondered why all structures weren't built this way, even back in Edra.

He continued forward into the town, leaving the dock in search of more Pastoran beauty. What he found did not disappoint. Vendors lined the edges of the dirt road, selling foreign goods and spices to men and women of all sorts and from all places. Sir Willam couldn't tell who was a local and who had come to sell their goods or escape their troubles. *Or perhaps there are others like me*, he thought, *who have come to solve someone else's problems*.

He ventured through Biverna without urgency, taking it all in. He saw a band of dwarves riding big, shaggy-maned dogs through the streets. He moved his hand to rest on the hilt of his sword, eyeing them as he went. Then he saw a woman selling potions and throwing frog eyes into a steaming black cauldron, and he looked around incredulously at the people walking by.

Nobody seemed bothered by her display of witchcraft, no soldiers or guards rushed in to arrest her. Then he saw a couple who had seven arms between them, sitting on a roadside bench and holding hands while eating cheese and bread and combing each other's hair all at the same time.

Among all the wonders, the thing that kept stealing his eye was the green mountain ahead. Looming protectively over the town, the mountain was enormous, covered in trees and shrubbery. Sir Willam glanced at it so often that by the time he had finally found the sign for the inn, a hexagonal plaque of wood with a depiction of the mountain carved into it and painted, he had lost any interest in what he might find inside. The door opened in front of him regardless, by his own hand, and his legs pulled him in.

The inn smelled of strong ale and roasted chicken, and much like the streets it was crowded with color. The women wore bright pink and emerald green, ocean blue, and dandelion yellow. Their dresses flowed and twirled with them as they danced. Some hung loose and slid gracefully with every step, while others clung tight to their bodies, forcing the knight to keep his mind on task. He focused instead on the men, thinking perhaps he might see Yevnir among them. Some of them wore odd, feathered hats or tall pointy hats, and only a few wore no hats at all.

For the most part, the pointy-hatted fellows and the no-hatted fellows moved stiffly in comparison to the women, who seemed to be the most free-spirited people Sir Willam had ever seen. They all danced to the drumming and windpipes of a Pastoran band, the kind of music that was impossible not to at least nod your head to, although Sir Willam surely tried. Even as he fought the urge to dance, he remembered what he was there for, and he searched the faces to find his friend. Yevnir was nowhere to be seen, however.

Heading toward the barkeep, he pushed past a slender, feather-hatted man dancing whimsically on his own, then ran into a pair of dancing Eastern Islanders, the first he had ever seen. The man was a head taller than him, and the woman half a head, but both had the same dark skin and silver-green eyes. The mask that the woman wore gave away their ethnicity.

It was of a solid white and glossy material; red lines ran vertically over its surface and small black and yellow triangles made patterns in between. The eye holes were horizontal diamonds, lined with black paint, and inside them her eyes glowed green. Sir Willam had heard from an Edran lord many years ago that everyone of status in the Eastern Islands wore painted masks. The lord had said it with some disdain, but seeing it in person, Sir Willam was enthralled.

"Dance with us, Edran man," the woman said, spinning under the arm of her partner. Her dress was not of the loose variety, but Sir Willam hardly noticed because of the sharpness of her eyes and the oddly seductive enchantment of her mask.

"Your dancing partner is far more elegant than I," Sir Willam shouted over the beating of the drums. "Besides, I am supposed to ask you that question."

Her partner swung her again and let go, sending her spiraling into Sir Willam's arms. "Not here," she said, her mask coming an inch from his face. "I choose my partner here. He is a pirate, and you are a knight, no?"

"Sir Willam Hornsby." He put an arm around her waist and took her hand in the other, mimicking the dance he'd seen them do, only pulling her a little closer. Any feeling of guilt for stealing this dance subsided as soon as he saw her last partner join with another pair. The knight glanced quickly over at the barkeep, whom he had intended to question about Yevnir's whereabouts. *Yevnir can wait*, he thought.

"I am Tessara," said the woman.

"Are you here for business, my lady? I wouldn't have expected an Eastern Islander to speak the language of the continent."

"Yes. It is the common language in Pastora also. I learn it for here."

Sir Willam chuckled. "You learned it." He could see she was smiling by the way her eyes squinted slightly behind her mask.

"I *learned* it. Yes. Not very good." Although he had pointed out her mistake, her reply held no hint of embarrassment. Still, the knight tried to console her.

"It's not so easy to learn another land's tongue. Otherwise, I might speak . . ."

"Ahkovan."

Sir Willam spun her. The music was beginning to settle so they no longer had to shout. "You're from Ahkova?" There were five so-called Eastern Islands: Boncopa, Ahkova, Sivelli, Pueria, and Sroma. Ahkova was the smallest and poorest of them all. He had heard it called the poor sister of Boncopa.

Tessara nodded, pointed at an empty table by the wall, and pulled him by the hand. As quickly as they sat, a barmaid came and poured two cups of sweet-smelling red wine. Tessara pulled the mask over her head and set it face down on the table, freeing long braids to fall down her back and in front of her shoulder.

The mask could not have revealed a mystery so pleasant to the knight. Her skin was smooth and her lips full. When she smiled, little dimples formed on both sides of her mouth.

"What were you doing dancing with a pirate, my lady?" Sir Willam asked.

She sipped her wine then rested her hands on the table. "Would you still call me lady if you knew I was a pirate too?"

Sir Willam shrugged, picked up his cup, and thought, *To hell with honor.*

"I would call you whatever pleases you. Lady, pirate, it makes no difference to me."

"Lady Pirate," she said, "you can say both for me. 'Yes, Lady Pirate. Take me to dance, Lady Pirate.' I like that very much."

"I have never met a lady pirate. Are you as fierce as the pirates in the Paritine? Those I have met, and if you are anything like them, then I should really be intrigued."

"I am!" she exclaimed. "I am fiercer than all."

"What is it like?" Willam asked. "Pirating, I mean."

"It is freedom," she said with a twinkle in her eyes. "No vows for us." Her "r"s rolled, remnants of her native tongue, and the knight was equally excited by what she said as he was by the way she said it. He felt he could speak to her as if their two professions weren't opposites, as if he hadn't taken vows to protect the innocents she stole from. Perhaps because he couldn't imagine that she ever stole from Edrans.

"Do you ever feel bad for taking from them?" He shifted in his seat, suddenly worried his question would offend her. "I only mean to say," he continued, "does it weigh on you, what you do?"

She smiled, revealing a gold tooth that reflected a bit of firelight. "Do you always do the right thing, Sir Willam?"

"I try to, genuinely, though it is not always as clear as I would like it to be."

The look she gave him made him eager to blur the lines further, to have the chance to justify doing something wrong for a change.

"My crew is family," she said, sipping her wine. "I provide. Is it wrong to provide?"

Nothing she said could be wrong. That was the way he felt looking at her, but touching the bronze brooch at his throat, feeling the spiked branches of the ornamental tree by his heart, he made the subconscious choice to change the subject rather than give her an answer.

"Does your ship have a name, Lady Pirate?"

"*Sivkharadiv*," she said proudly, "but it is easier for westerners to say *Sivkara*. Your tongue doesn't like suffix of 'div.'"

He nodded with a slight smirk, glad for the westernized

version. Hearing her pronounce the ship's name, he had tried to watch her mouth to see how she rolled her tongue at the "r" and how her tongue had seemed to poke through her teeth at "div" and couldn't imagine himself recreating it.

"What does it mean?" he asked.

"There is no good word to match. It means we are what you look for when you cannot find. When you have lost a thing. Something like this."

"Interesting," he said. "And what if you are looking for something you didn't lose?"

"Why would you do this? If you haven't lost a thing, you don't need to find it."

"What if it's something you want but have never had? Is there a word for that in Ahkovan?"

"Hmm. I see. There are a few words for this. Sidikadiv, mostiladil, Tessara . . ." She grinned, and they fell into laughter together. They both looked down at their cups for a while and listened to the band as they drank, swapping glances from time to time, a smile here and there.

"May I ask you something?"

"Yes," Tessara said excitedly.

"Why do you wear the mask of an aristocrat?"

"Hmm," Tessara put a finger to her chin and smiled. "You have a king in Edra, yes?"

"Of course. King Gramon Antaeus."

"If you could wear his crown, would you?"

"No," Sir Willam chuckled, taking another drink. "Knighthood is hard enough; kingship would be torture."

"Maybe we are different, then."

"I suspect we might be more similar than you think."

"How so?"

"Do you want to be a pirate forever?"

"Yes. I told you this. It is freedom."

"Freedom for whom? You told me you have to provide. I

would say lack of responsibility is freedom, which makes you and I prisoners, filing away our shackles with wooden spoons."

Tessara grinned at this and looked away for a while. The two enjoyed the silence between them, and the music around them, until finally Tessara said, in a break between songs, "And what else for you?"

"What do you mean?"

"I am a lady and a pirate. You are a knight and what else?"

"You could say I am a brother, a friend, and a fisherman too."

Sir Willam shrugged and chugged the rest of his cup. "But I can be a pirate with you if you'd like to host me on your ship." He thought, even as he spoke, that he was out of practice with this sort of thing.

"Oh, you are very forward, Sir Willam," she said, playfully rolling her eyes. "Maybe you could be a true pirate, but you're an Edran man. Your gods would punish you for pirating, no?"

"There are exceptions to the rules, even to the vows of knighthood. This is one. It is written somewhere in the Sydia, I'm sure."

"You have not read it?" Tessara leaned over the table, intrigued.

"There are things more important than old books when you're in the presence of a woman such as yourself. If it doesn't say a knight can turn pirate for beauty in the Sydia, then I don't want to read it. Do you believe in the gods in Ahkova?"

"Some," Tessara said. "None of yours."

Sir Willam shook his head vehemently. "Not mine, theirs. All the other Edrans'. I worship something else entirely." The mention of Edrans reminded him once more that he came here to find one. "Have you seen another Edran man around? He is a merchant named Yevnir Goldleaf. He's a bit shorter than me, curly black hair and brown eyes. Talks too much, never tells the truth."

Tessara squinted and pursed her lips, then tilted her head to the side. “Goldleaf—yes. My crewmate finds him for you. Uh, brings him for you—to him.” She finished her sentence with a sort of proud bounce in her seat and then waved her hand at her dance partner to catch his attention.

The other Eastern Islander hurried over to their table and towered over them so much that Sir Willam had to crane his neck to look him in the eyes. Tessara and her dance partner spoke to each other in their language for what seemed like an entire minute.

Finally, he looked at Sir Willam and said, “Follow.”

The knight turned to Tessara. “That was quick. Maybe we can talk for a while longer. I’m sure Yevnir can wait awhile.”

“Go. Find your friend, knight. Maybe he’s in trouble.”

“Oh, of that I have no doubt. Will I see you again, my lady?”

“Only if you’re lucky, Sir Willam.”

He smiled and reached for her hand. Bowing his head, he kissed it in the space between her silver and gold rings and her thin gold bracelet. “It is a good thing, then, that we’ve met in the land of luck.”

CHAPTER THREE

The Pastoran drummers banged heavily on their instruments, a lutist plucked his strings, and the bard sang his melody loud and fast, the muscles in his neck straining with effort.

Sir Willam left Lady Tessara at the table, following her companion to the door. As they budged through the dense crowd of dancers, the knight looked back sporadically to catch another glimpse of the Ahkovan beauty.

When they came out into the street, they found that a group of children had taken over with a ball game. A small, tan-skinned boy sat against the wall of the inn to Sir Willam's left, crying and holding his scraped knee.

"Give me a second, if you don't mind," Sir Willam said to the pirate, who nodded and leaned against the wall with folded arms.

He squatted down next to the boy. "Are you alright?"

"No," the boy cried, "they threw me on the ground."

"Why would they do that?"

"They said I couldn't play. It's because I'm a Simerian! They don't like me, but as soon as I'm done crying, I will take the ball from them and score."

Sir Willam smiled and rubbed the boy's shaggy black hair. "I have no doubt you will, little warrior. But look, we're talking, and you're done crying already."

The little boy's eyes widened with realization, and he pushed himself to his feet. Sir Willam brushed the dirt from his cloth robe.

"Are you a knight?" the boy asked, looking slack-jawed at the sword on his hip.

"I am. My name is Sir Willam Hornsby. What's yours?" he said, reaching out to shake the boy's hand.

The little Simerian took his hand and shook it proudly. "I am Ardee. I don't have a family name like you do. I'm an orphan. Is your family rich? Do they live in a castle?"

The knight chuckled. "No, no. Not at all. Can you keep a secret?" he asked, looking around. As soon as the boy nodded, Sir Willam continued, "I am an orphan too, and I came from a village even smaller than this little town. I do have brothers though, so I was never alone. Do you have anybody to look after you?"

Ardee grimaced and stuck his hands in his pockets.

"There is a place near here where people like me sleep. They give us food sometimes. Wait, if you are an orphan like me, how do you have a family name? Did you know your parents?"

"No, I was too young when they died. But people don't have family names where I'm from, not unless they're lords or very rich."

"So then how did you get one?"

"I made it up."

"You made it up?"

"Shh. Only you can know."

The boy leaned in and talking almost in a whisper said, "Can I make up a family name too?"

"Yes," answered Sir Willam, "but first you must take that

ball back and show them that you can play as well as anyone else."

With a toothy grin and excited eyes, the kid sprinted past the knight and put himself back in the game, chasing the ball with newfound energy and seemingly forgetting the scrape on his knee. Sir Willam smirked as he turned to follow the Ahkovan pirate to the mountainside.

As they left the town of Biverna and began their ascent up the lush green mountain, the knight tried to make conversation with his Ahkovan guide.

"Poor child. I can't imagine being such a lonely outsider. I'm sure there are other Simerians on the island, but a boy should grow up in his homeland, his motherland—especially if he doesn't have a mother. Don't you think?" The Ahkovan didn't so much as nod.

Sir Willam tried again with another topic. "I apologize for my behavior with Lady Tessara. I did not mean to steal your dance," he said, stepping over a fallen tree.

"Captain," said the pirate.

"Captain? Ah, she is the captain of your ship?"

"Captain and sister."

Sister? the knight thought. *She could've mentioned that*. But he said, "Oh, wonderful!"

And the pirate responded, "Yes."

Silence followed.

They walked a gradual wooded incline and climbed when they got to a steep rock face. Willam's calves burned and his forehead dripped stinging beads of sweat into his eyes. The silence forced him to think about every painful step. The pain made him miss his old horse, Baron, although he wasn't sure he would even be capable of making this climb.

Once they had pushed far enough up the mountain into the forest, that silent tension subsided into a welcomed enchantment.

The knight felt as though he was alone in the forest and at the same time as though he and the pirate were in the company of a presence they could not see, like they were walking blindfolded through a crowd.

Birds and squirrels darted about in the trees, but it was not their presence that made him feel surrounded. This feeling was so intense, and he was so sure of it, that he half expected to find a gathering of people at the top of every ridge. But when they climbed over one of these steep ridges, where the land stretched flat and the trees were scarce, they found only a meadow.

Here, purple fireweed, orange and red tiger lilies, and little yellow buttercups almost outnumbered the blades of tall grass surrounding them. In the center of the meadow, there was a small pool of water, more puddle than pond, which quenched the thirst of a slender, almond-colored elk.

The creature bowed its long neck to the water's edge, lapping up water under a twenty-pointed crown of thick, wood-colored antlers. Like the stone structures in Biverna, there were patches of dark-green moss growing from the elk's crown and spiderwebs connecting each antler with the one beside it.

The pirate reached for a dagger, pulling it gently and slowly from its sheath. The elk had not seen them yet.

Sir Willam grabbed his arm. "I won't dine on so rare a beast," he said.

The pirate shrugged and sheathed his dagger. The sound caused the elk's eyes to dart toward them, and it took off into the woods far to their right.

"Good meat," said the pirate, shaking his head.

"I'm sure," Sir Willam agreed. "How far are we from Yevnir's cabin?"

The pirate pointed up and to the left of the meadow, where they could barely make out a clearing. Sir Willam sighed and the two continued on. It occurred to him that the man he was traveling with was, in fact, a pirate. It could have been because he didn't possess the same distractions as his sister—the lips, the dimples, the hair—that the significance of his profession only came this late in their journey, but he started to watch him more closely after the thought came.

When they finally reached the cabin, the knight was shocked to see it looked nothing like the other structures of Pastora. In fact, it was not a cabin at all but rather an entire house in the style of Bordaen architecture with light-stone brick for the walls and a red-clay-tiled roof. *He was not exaggerating in his letter*, Sir Willam thought. *He really does miss Bordae.*

"Yevnir!" the knight shouted, putting his hands at the sides of his mouth. "I'm here, Yev. It's me! It's Will." He was elated by the thought of seeing his friend again after so many years and expected to see his big smiling face pop out of one of the windows.

When no reply came and no face appeared, the knight looked at the pirate worryingly, and the pirate shook his head. "Not home," he said.

Sir Willam hurried to the door, knocked, then slapped his hand against the wood to nudge the door open. "Yev!" he shouted, stepping inside. Again, there was no reply.

Inside, parchments and scrolls were strewn all over the floor, chests and coffers were turned over and emptied, and there were holes right through the middle of every hanging painting. Sir Willam squatted down to rummage through a pile of scrolls. Business agreements, for the most part. A chart of supplies procured by Yevnir for the Hollow Mountain Inn, a bill of sale for a home Yevnir had owned in town, and a few letters of employment for the builders of the house they stood in.

There was nothing to imply whom Yevnir had scammed this time or who did this to his home.

The knight scanned the room, going from the kitchen

ahead of them, with its brick oven, and knocked over table and chairs, to the spiral staircase to his left, which led up into a loft. At the bottom of the stairs there was a bend in the metal railing. "He must've been thrown into it. Look, there is a—"

Sir Willam turned to a face full of a scimitar pommel, sending him right toward the dent in the railing. His nose stung and he immediately felt the flow of blood running over his lips and down his chin. Falling to his back, he rolled sideways to avoid a crashing boot.

The pirate's eyes glimmered with excitement as he wound back his curved sword and leaped forward at the knight, who pulled his dagger in time to slash and force the pirate back a step. Willam jumped to his feet, drawing his sword with his free hand.

"What are you doing? You led me here to kill me?"

The two faced each other square, the massive pirate with his scimitar and the knight with his dagger in one hand and his broadsword in the other.

"You trust too easy," said the pirate with a wicked smile.

"Is this because I danced with your sister?" the knight asked. "Because I've already apologized."

They circled each other now, stepping slowly around the debris of the torn-up house. "Yevnir," the pirate explained, "the Goldleaf."

"I see. He made a fool of you and your crew. I should've known. Where is he? Is he dead?"

The pirate sneered and charged, swinging wildly. Sir Willam ducked the swipe, letting the railing take the hit in place of his head. He blocked another with his broadsword and kicked his opponent's leg right under the knee. The pirate's knee gave and crumpled inward. He winced and screamed and swung from a kneeling position, but Sir Willam stood out of range.

"I won't kill you, pirate," Sir Willam said, sheathing his

dagger but not his sword, "as long as you tell me where my friend is."

The pirate craned his neck and leaped off of one leg, taking one more swing at the knight. Sir Willam smacked the scimitar out of the pirate's hand and hit him square in the face with the pommel of his broadsword, right in the same spot where he had been hit. Holding his nose, the pirate fell to the ground atop a scattered pile of parchment and a chest made of orange wood with iron center bands.

"For a tall man, you really don't know how to use your reach, you know. Shame on you. I'll have to tell your sister that the Paritine pirates are the fiercer. Now, where is Yevnir?"

The knight let his sword hover in front of the pirate's throat.

"Dead," spat the pirate. "Me."

Sir Willam shook his head. "You didn't kill him. You were searching for something." He gestured toward the torn-apart room, the scattered scrolls, and the ripped-up paintings. "And I don't think you ever found it. What? Nothing to say? Did you think I would lead you to his treasure? No, not you. You don't have the brain for it. Your sister is the one searching. But what for?"

Now the pirate squirmed, and the knight thwacked him on the forehead with the flat side of his blade. "Here's what you're going to do. I'm going to give you a head start down that mountain. Let's say . . . an hour. And you're going to run and tumble down it back to your sister. Tell her I don't want any trouble with your crew. I just want my friend back, and whatever land, property, or gold Yevnir scammed her out of will be hers upon his safe return to me. Do you understand?"

The pirate nodded, a bitter expression on his face. Sir Willam felt he hadn't quite absorbed the point.

"If I catch you, I'll kill you. Then I'll kill your sister. Then the rest of your crew. Sound fair? Good. Time starts now."

The pirate struggled to his feet and hurried to the door with a hobble in his step. He pushed it open with one hand and held his leg with the other. Sir Willam followed him out, sword in hand, and watched him struggle down through the wooded mountainside with no intention to follow. Once he was out of sight, Sir Willam went back inside the house, continuing his search for clues.

There has to be something, he thought, throwing a scroll over his shoulder. After a while of sifting through documents, searching the loft above and the cellar below, he returned to the main room and set a chair upright to have a seat. Before sitting, he undid his belt and set it, sword and all, on the table next to him. Stepping toward his chair, his foot turned over a parchment on the floor enough to reveal the corner of a hasty sketch. He knelt down to examine it and found a strange drawing of what looked like a squirrel. He picked it up, smiled at its absurdity, set it on top of a turned-over chest, then finally took a rest.

The knight let his mind take him through any number of possible scenarios that could've led to his meeting with the Ahkovan pirates, or rather Yevnir's meeting with them.

"There can be no doubt that he is to blame for this whole mess," Sir Willam said to himself, "and if they haven't yet beaten him to a pulp, then maybe I should once I find him."

A knock came at the front window. Not the knock of a hand but a single, startling sound, like somebody had thrown a rock at the glass. Sir Willam sprang to his feet, reaching for his sword belt, but paused when he heard another *ting* on the glass and looked to see an acorn bouncing off it. A few feet in front of the window, the assailant stood at the tip of a pine branch.

It was a squirrel. Only instead of brown or black fur, it was orange with black stripes, like the design of a tiger's coat, and it was, Sir Willam thought, adorably small, even more so than the average squirrel.

Sir Willam picked up the sketch from the lid of the chest

and held it out in front of him so that he could see both the drawing and the real thing through the window. "You are a lot of things, Yevnir," he said aloud, "but an artist is not one of them." As he went to sit back down, the squirrel threw another nut at the window. "By the Druid!" he shouted.

This time he grabbed his sword belt and fastened it as he stormed toward the front door.

"Alright! I don't care how rare a creature you are, squirrel. You will leave me alone!" He pushed the door open and heard the crunch of a nut under his boot. Looking down, he saw a curious line of acorns in front of him and followed it with his eyes all the way into the woods ahead. Turning to the pine where the squirrel had been throwing his projectiles from, he saw that the little creature had disappeared.

"Oh no!" he declared loudly. "If you think you're going to lead me into an ambush of all your squirrel friends, you are severely mistaken. You won't be throwing any more nuts my way!"

He turned to go back inside, and an acorn whacked him in the back of the head, fast as an arrow. The knight drew his sword, furious, and stomped back the other way, following the trail of nuts into the mountain forest.

CHAPTER FOUR

The longer he followed the trail, the greater the variety of nuts he encountered. There were hazelnuts, walnuts, and pecans; marrow nuts, which he'd thought were only native to the east of Edra; and a few varieties of nuts he had never seen. In some places, they were so spread out that Sir Willam thought the trail had ended. But every time he lost it, he would see the tiger-colored squirrel sprint from a bush and scurry up a tree or jump from limb to limb overhead, and he would find a new variety of nut in the spot where he'd seen it. One time there was a yellow nut that looked like a tiny banana, another a purple nut that he almost mistook for a bean.

Finally, after he'd followed the nuts through a mile of forest and climbed to an even higher part of the mountain, there came an end to the trail. On a small plateau thick with brush and tall, vine-riddled trees, there were the ruins of an old tower barely poking out of the thicket.

It was so covered in vines that it looked like the mountain was slowly swallowing it whole, like how a snake swallows a rabbit. He remembered Tren briefly. In his mind he saw a flashing image of the boy being devoured by a siren in the darkness of the ocean's depths. The siren unhinged its jaw, its red gills fluttering to the sides, and latched on to the top of Tren's head. The image was too painful to hold, so he buried it in the back of his mind and refocused on the tower.

The entrance was the only part of the tower that could be easily made out from where Sir Willam stood, and that was only because it had been recently opened. The vines that once covered the doorway had been cut, and although he could make out rusted hinges, whatever door that had been there had rotten away long ago.

The sun was setting by the time Sir Willam found this little tower, and it had been a long and tiresome day. So, despite being led here by a mischievous squirrel and half expecting to find an army of its kin ready to gnaw him to pieces inside, all he could think of was making a fire and settling down to bed. When he ducked into the passageway, pushing through vines that hung from a ceiling of cracked stone, and entered the tight courtyard, he immediately set out a spot for himself to sleep and set to work on building that fire.

When he was cozy, or as cozy as possible on stone ruins in a foreign land, he let his eyes close and his mind drift off to sleep. He used his cloak for a blanket and his satchel for a pillow. The gentle crackle of the fire and its warmth on his cheek lulled him straight into a dream, the kind so real that when he awoke, he wasn't sure which was the dream and which was reality.

The moon shone down into the courtyard with its dull blue light, and a squirrel that looked oddly like a tiger perched on a stone in front of him, chewing greedily on the rounded edges of a gold coin.

He scooted back and fumbled for his broadsword. "What are you, creature?"

The squirrel stopped its gnawing on the coin and looked up, revealing beady bright-yellow eyes and perky triangular ears. Then it turned and scurried into a dark doorway. Sir

Willam stood and lit a torch to follow it. He hurriedly descended a spiral staircase with his torch in his hand and his sword at his hip.

The stone in the stairway was smooth and light, like limestone, and there were no cracks in it. There were no vines or weeds growing from the walls like there were on the surface of the structure. *This area of the tower must've been sealed*, thought the knight. Before he could ask himself the question of who unsealed it, he came into an open corridor.

On one side of the room was a row of stone chests, their lids lying next to them on the floor or behind them in the space between the chests and the wall. The knight peered into each, holding up his torch as he leaned over them. One after another he found them empty, until looking into the last of them he saw the squirrel jutting back and forth and scratching at the stone.

"What are you after?"

The creature spun as if chasing its own tail and then scuttered up the stone and out of the chest, dashing between Sir Willam's legs toward the wall behind him. The knight whirled to keep up with it, the torch fire in his hand flickering as he waved it around him. It stopped in front of the wall opposite the chests. For a moment, it stood on its hind legs and stared at the cobweb-covered wall.

Sir Willam stepped toward it, expecting his movement to frighten the squirrel, but it stayed still, hardly noticing his presence. Walking right up next to it, so that the knight and the squirrel looked at the same wall side by side, he slowly waved his torch in front of him.

Beneath the webs, although obscured, was an etching engraved in the stone. When he made out the head of a human figure and the sharp edge of a sword in the etching, he began tearing and swatting at the thick layers of spider webs until finally, illuminated by torch fire, the knight and the squirrel gazed upon the depiction of a great battle.

There were two sides. A group of armored men sporting shields, swords, and spears were on their front feet, leaning into their shields and charging into battle. The other side was an assortment of beasts, even more odd than the tiger-striped squirrel by Sir Willam's left foot or the elk he had seen drinking in the meadow. No two were the same. There were men who had the lower body of a horse or a goat. There was a woman with the head of a lioness, and a lioness with the head of a woman, and there were giant folk towering over them all. There was a dog with three heads and there was a man with the head of a bull.

The beasts too were charging into battle, but not all of them. Half were running away from the armored men toward a row of trees that looked like they hadn't been finished, with pointy branches that had no leaves, as if the stone mason ran out of time to detail them. He thought for a second that they looked familiar, like the horn trees from the village he grew up in, then thought against it. *They couldn't be*, he said to himself.

Sir Willam studied the engravings with wonder. They had been chiseled so fine and preserved so well that he could see the expressions on the faces of the humans and the beasts. The human at the forefront of the charge looked angry, his mouth wide open and his sword high in the air. The beasts looked terrified. Even a giant, who looked as though she could eat the humans who charged her, appeared scared. Her hand was extended in front of her, a spear sticking into her palm that looked more like an arrow. But her face, even in the limits of a stone etching, still displayed her terror.

The etching ran almost the full length of the wall, so to get to the unfinished trees, Sir Willam had to walk and continue tearing down the webs. Swiping away at one of the last bits of web on the right side of the stone engraving, close to the trees where the beasts were escaping to, he blew the dust from the crevices of an unknown figure. It was a short, hooded man, standing beside the forest with open arms, seemingly welcoming the beasts into the forest.

"Why have you brought me here?" Sir Willam looked down at the squirrel, who had followed him along the wall. "Did you know my friend?" He squatted next to it, holding the torch above their heads. "Did you bring Yevnir here too? Is that why the chests are empty?"

The tiger-striped squirrel looked up at him with blank yellow eyes.

"Lot of help you are," Sir Willam said. Then, stroking his chin, he thought, *Why am I here, Yevnir? What did you do?* He pulled the letter from his waist pouch and unfolded it.

Skimming through, he came upon the part that read, "I am in a bit of a jam here on the island. One I cannot free myself of alone. I need your help. That is all I can say on the matter. You will know why if you make the journey."

"Well, I am here!" he shouted, and with a frustrated sigh he threw the letter on the floor. The squirrel stared up at him, tilting its head to the side. "Do not look at me like that, creature. You would be angry too if you were me. You've never had a friend pull you across the sea to save them?" Again, the squirrel stared at him blankly.

"You are a useless companion. Do you know that? I'd rather you had led me into a squirrel ambush, as I thought you would. At least then I'd have something to kill."

The knight stomped away toward the stairs, leaving the squirrel and the engraving and all the empty chests behind him. But when he had climbed the first few steps of the spiral stone staircase, right before turning the corner, he heard a noise from below—a crumpling, ripping noise—and turning back, he saw the squirrel eating the letter.

"First gold and now parchment? Do you eat everything but nuts?"

Curiously, the squirrel laid the letter down after eating only one corner. Sir Willam squinted and walked back to pick it up, but before he could get to it, the squirrel took off, bounding past him and up the stairs so quickly that Sir Willam barely had time to turn before it had disappeared. He sprinted after it.

Coming to the top of the stairs, he saw the end of its fluffy tail turning into the passageway to leave the tower. He ran to where he had slept and grabbed his satchel and cloak, throwing them on as he chased after it. Torch in hand, he ducked into the passage. Pushing through vines and tripping over debris, he went to the beam of moonlight that marked his exit. His head came out into the open and . . .

Wham! He fell back into the passageway, unsure what had hit him.

His torch flew from his hands and his vision went blurry. He squinted and tried to focus on the figures that converged on him. His eyes closed and reopened again, and he saw a masked figure leaning over his body. "Shhh," the figure said, a finger to the mouth, "go to sleep, knight."

And his eyes closed, his vision dropping from moonlight into blackness.

CHAPTER FIVE

When he woke, he was falling, bouncing actually, as if he were going headfirst down a hill—no, a mountain. There was a sharp throbbing pain at the top of his skull. His body was curved into an upside-down "u," all his blood rushing to his head. Then he felt a hand resting on his upper back. He saw only blackness still. Groaning, he tried to shift his weight but found he was stuck.

"Where am I?"

A woman's voice answered. "You're down a mountain, knight. Still climbing down. Don't worry. We'll take you to your friend."

"Tessara? Is that you?" He wiggled his hands and found that, to his surprise, they weren't bound.

"No. Captain is waiting for you on the ship."

Another voice, this time a man's, said, "We bring you to the captain. You happy?"

I think this fool forgot to bind my wrists, thought the knight, pulling the blindfold from his eyes as he bounced. Despite his current situation and the raging headache at the top of his skull, Sir Willam still managed to force a rebellious smile.

"Never been happier. Thank you for the ride." He had been captured before, but never without having his hands tied.

"You're—"

"Quiet!" interrupted the woman.

Sir Willam laughed. "Yes. Silence, brute. Me and the lady are conversing."

"You be quiet too, knight."

"No, I don't think so. I don't think so at all. I have much more to say, actually. I'd like to know what state I'll be finding my friend in when we get to this ship of yours. For another, I'd like to ask if you *really* think a knight would travel alone, as if I do not have a company of men waiting for my return to our ship." The knight gave an obnoxious scoff at the end of this to really sell his bluff. "Thirdly, before you answer, I demand you get this carriage of a man under me some sort of perfume. There is an abominable stench coming from the pits of his arms."

"Stupid knight!" the brute said in a deep, offended voice.

Sir Willam whacked the top of the brute's ass with an open palm and yelled, "Shut up, donkey!"

Next thing he knew, his legs flew over his head, and his body landed hard in the sloped earth, his face buried in the leaves and stems of some woodland brush. He spit out a mouthful of weeds and started to push himself to his feet when he felt a hard kick to his ribs. Keeling over to his back, he waved his hand in front of him to show his submission.

"I yield! I yield!" he said, coughing and holding his ribs. In the brief moment he was there on the ground, he surveyed the area around him and the people who had taken him captive. He noted that the woman had his sword belt and his satchel. Then, smirking and closing his eyes, he said, "You have bested me. Now if only you could best your own stench."

The pirate grabbed him by the collar and shook him furiously, as if he were a child.

"Enough, Jakka!" the woman yelled. "We have to keep moving."

Jakka forced the blindfold back over Sir Willam's eyes then threw him over his shoulder, and he settled back into his clavicle saddle.

"It was a rude thing to say," he admitted. "You don't stink as bad as all that, Jakka the brute. I'm sorry for saying so. Can we be friends again?"

Jakka grunted, and Sir Willam took that as a yes. They continued down the mountain for another half hour until the slope met flat land. "Are you taking me back through Biverna, dear captors? To the docks?"

"No," the woman griped.

"Right, then. Well, let's hurry up. My legs are getting tired."

As he bounced upon Jakka's shoulder, his ribs sore from the rough ride, he thought about making an escape several times. There was nothing stopping him from climbing off. His hands were free, and although Jakka was much bigger and stronger than him, he was also heavyset with a barrel of a belly, so Sir Willam was confident he could wriggle free and the big man would not catch him. The idea swirled around in his mind until finally he put it to rest and thought, *They are taking me right to Yev*.

After a short walk on flat ground, about the same distance as his walk through the town of Biverna the day before, although much quieter, he began to hear the splashing of waves against the shore. Then came the sharp smell of salt in the air, and the kerplunking of a boat rocking with the tide. Pulling the blindfold from his eyes, he saw they were passing between two almost identical rocky hills. At the top of the hill to his right was a single leafless tree, and on it he could make out a flicker of orange passing from branch to branch.

It's the squirrel, he thought. *What is it doing here?*

He tried to look forward to see the source of the kerplunking, but he couldn't lift his head enough to do it. In a second, he was thrown onto the hard planks of a little rowboat, and the point of a scimitar was being pressed against his throat. The female pirate yanked his blindfold off his face and said, "To the front. Row."

When he turned, he saw the *Sivkara* in all its glory. The ship was massive with two huge sails that were closed and a world's worth of painted shields lining the rails, boasting of, Sir Willam assumed, all the places they had successfully raided. It wasn't until he started pulling with the oars that he recognized an Edran coat of arms on one of the shields. It was an oak tree, the sigil of Woodsworth.

He was probably the only person from Horntree, the village he grew up in, who would recognize the sigil. It would have amused him that even the symbol of a city so close to his birthplace would be unrecognizable to his brothers, but then he realized what it meant. These pirates had been to Edra, raided his own shores, and he had flirted with their captain rather than killing her.

Beyond the shields, the knight could scarcely make out a few pirates pointing at him from the main deck. He followed their heads to the stern of the ship, where he hoped to see Captain Tessara, but instead his attention was taken by a black flag that waved in the wind from the crow's nest atop the back sail, and he looked back to make out its design.

A shiver went down his spine as he saw the patterned white mask he had seen Tessara wearing in the Hollow Mountain Inn, staring at him from the center of the black flag. He felt as though it were her staring at him, and the green within the eyeholes now unsettled him rather than pulling him in.

Turning his neck slightly toward shore, he thought about taking his chances with Jakka and the female pirate behind him, but the point of her scimitar poked into his back, and he faced forward again. He was forced by that same point of the scimitar to climb a rope ladder when their rowboat finally met the *Sivkara*.

Once they were on the deck, he was brought to his knees. The crew of Ahkovan pirates stopped their work to gather around him, letting mops fall and finishing off knots in a hurry. To his left, on the stern side, the cabin door opened, and out limped the pirate he had fought in Yevnir's mountainside manor. His leg was splinted with iron beams and leather straps running up to his mid-thigh. The pirate walked toward him with the help of a cane, and to Sir Willam's surprise he was smiling. Somehow this was the first time the knight noticed his dreadful yellow teeth, which seemed to match his little gold hoop earrings.

"Old friend!" the knight exclaimed jovially. "What a pleasure it is to see you. But I hope you don't mind if I could have a word with your sister?"

The pirate steadied himself and reached out with a long arm to slap the knight with the back of his bony knuckle. Sir Willam's lip split. He popped to his feet, but Jakka shoved him right back to his knees, this time grabbing his arms and holding them behind his back.

The knight licked his bleeding lip. "I love the taste of my own blood," he declared, halting his attempt to wriggle free. "Though I must admit I've never tried anybody else's. Maybe yours will be the first. Yes, I think it will. Then you, Jakka the donkey. I have a feeling your blood will taste like butter and honey."

A few cackles came from the crew, then they all broke out in laughter. Sir Willam looked up at them with a red smile on his face, unsure if they were laughing at his calling Jakka fat or a donkey. When he started to chuckle with them, however, their laughter faded, and their heads turned to the stairs of the quarterdeck.

Sir Willam frowned and looked to see what they were

staring at. From the bottom step, a boot landed and then another. Lady Tessara, her long braids swaying to one side of her shoulder and then back into place, commanded the silence she received. As she approached, she reached back and gathered her hair in both hands and tied it up so that nothing hung loose, a gesture that felt like the equivalent of someone rolling up their sleeves for a fight.

Sir Willam smiled nonetheless. "I told you we would see each other again in the land of luck, Lady Pirate."

"But we are not on land, Sir Willam. Here, I am just a pirate." Then she turned her head toward the crew and shouted something in Ahkovan. They all scurried back to whichever tasks they had previously been occupied with, leaving Jakka, the other female pirate, Tessara's brother, and Tessara with Sir Willam.

He cleared his throat for his next attempt at a lie. "I hope this does not spoil our chances. You should know I will not hold a grudge. Free me, and free my friend, and then you and I can pick up right where we left off."

"Your friend stole gold. Much gold from me. Treasures that we found. And he will not tell us where he put them."

"Yevnir is a very good liar," said the knight, "but he has never had great resolve. He did not squeal his secrets when you tortured him?"

"He has told us nothing. If you can make him, both will go free. But you will not be lucky with this lady pirate." This last statement was accompanied by a smirk, her dimples slightly breaking the perfect smoothness of her cheeks. *So Yevnir has been tortured*, thought the knight. *They will have to answer for that.*

"Bring me to him, and I will bring you to your gold," he said.

Tessara flicked her finger, and Jakka raised Sir Willam to his feet then turned him around and began to tie his wrists. "Now you tie my wrists?" chuckled the knight. "Now that I am on a ship half a mile from the shore and surrounded by pirates, no less? Why now?"

"Because he wanted you to try," the woman stated.

Sir Willam frowned once again, looking from the woman back to Jakka. "Is that true, donkey?" The brute said nothing but responded with a wicked, toothy grin. *Then let me be glad I didn't*, thought the knight.

After his hands were bound, the woman opened a hatch near the bow of the ship and Jakka shoved him into it. He landed with a thud on stiff boards. The room was dark, and he could barely make out the back of it. Two rows of beams ran from the floor to the ceiling, and on every other one a sconce burned with dwindling light. Between some of the beams, rope hammocks swung with the rocking of the ship.

Jakka climbed down a short ladder that Sir Willam was not given the privilege of using, and upon setting his feet in the hull, he wrenched Sir Willam from the floor.

"Ready to see your friend?"

Sir Willam said nothing as Jakka pushed him toward the stern of the ship. Stumbling forward through the hull, the iron bars of a cell became visible in the dull light.

"Will? Is that you?" A man squinted through the scarce light with bruised eyes and swollen cheeks. He poked his head through the bars as far as he could, grasping them with both hands to try to squeeze himself through. He wore a dark-yellow tunic that had seen better days. It was tattered and ripped at the sleeves, and blood splotches ran down from his collar to his midsection. "No, no, no," he whimpered.

Jakka threw Sir Willam to the ground and unsheathed his scimitar. He whipped the blunt side against Yevnir's hands and sent him to the ground, grabbing his knuckles in pain. Then he took a key from his belt and opened the cell.

"In," he ordered.

The knight stood shakily and walked forward, the point of Jakka's scimitar giving him no other option. When he was in, Jakka slammed the door and locked it.

"Happy now?" he proclaimed and walked away, his figure disappearing and reappearing with the light from the open hatch.

"I'm so sorry, Will," said Yevnir, his voice hoarse. "I never wanted to drag you into this, but I had no other choice." He sat against the back of the hull; his bare legs stretched out in front of him on the boards.

"You owe me answers, Yev."

"I know. I will tell you everything. How are you though? How have you been? It has been years. Your brothers? Are they doing well?"

"You don't care about my brothers. I am not sure you really care about me, otherwise I wouldn't be in a cell right now. I have come too far to hear you lie, so tell me why I'm here."

Yevnir sighed and ran his hands along his tunic to straighten the wrinkles. "We are not all cut out for a life of roaming and killing and saving the day, you know. I wish I were like you. I do. Alas, while your talent is with the sword, mine is with the voice. I have lied my way through this exciting life, but I swear this misfortune did not come of a lie. I found their treasure, along with the other treasures, and I relocated them. That's it. How was I supposed to know the pirates would come back for their loot? Most people who hide such things do it because they are in trouble. I found their cache and thought, 'Whoever hid this much gold must have made a lot of enemies.' Then I took a gamble, an unlucky one. Nobody had killed the pirates yet, and now I have paid the price for it."

"Unlucky?" Sir Willam shook his head. "You said the same thing about the debt collector in Bordae."

"Now, that *was* unlucky, Will! Four years I had been back in Bordae, and a debt collector happened to sit down to a game of dice with me. What are the chances? Of all the places in Edra, the debt collector happened to come to my little gambling tavern in Bordae and recognize my face."

"He was Bordaen. He lived in the city. You knew him."

"Well, yes, we grew up together, but that is beside the point. That's a traveling profession, isn't it? And what kind of debt collector gambles?"

"Yev . . ."

The Goldleaf looked back at Sir Willam earnestly. "Alright. I'm sorry. I've messed things up again, it seems. But it may not seem so in a few days. Let things play out, follow my lead, and I promise you will be happy you answered my call."

Yevnir winced and grabbed his cheek after he spoke, and Sir Willam saw the black and blue under his eye and the small cut above his cheekbone for the first time.

"Who did it?"

"This?" Yevnir shrugged. "One of the pirates. I never caught a name. It was Jakka who broke my tooth a few days ago though."

"And Tessara? Varro? How have they treated you?"

"The captain is not as harsh as she may seem. She only started pirating to support her family in Ahkova, and now she is in too deep to stop. She supports the whole crew and all their families and feels responsible for half of Ahkova now. The first mate, though, he is the real softie. Loves his sister and his family fiercely. Neither of them has laid a hand on me, really. It's only been a few crewmen who have come down here and tried to get the location out of me by force. Jakka is the worst of the pirates by far. He has a wife back home who detests him, and let's just say it isn't because he's stayed faithful to her during his pirating years."

"How do you know all of this?"

"When you do what I do, you learn to read people."

"Being a con man is not a profession."

"I am not a con man!" Yevnir sat up straight. "I'm an adventurer and a businessman, and when you're adventuring and . . . businessing, you need to know how to read people."

Sir Willam raised an eyebrow and stared at his friend.

"Alright, Varro told me everything. He came to me one night and practically begged me to tell him where the treasure was. He said he had a child on the way and needed the gold. He's come to talk to me several times since."

"And what did you say?"

"When? Oh, when he asked about the gold? I said I wished I could help him but couldn't because I didn't know where it was. He was the only one I said that to who believed me."

"Because you meant it?"

"No, because I sold the lie better. I didn't wish I could help him. Will, these are pirates. You saw the Edran shields out there. They've raided our shores. Their stash was filled with Antaeus silvers and golds. There were even Gramon golds."

Willam knew of these gold coins but had barely ever seen any. They were first minted three years prior, in 4900 P.S. (Post Shatter), and he had only seen a few in circulation. They were worth ten of the old Coldon golds. This meant the pirates had been raiding, or at least stealing from, Edran ships within the last few years.

"I don't feel bad for taking from pirates, my friend," Yevnir continued, "and you shouldn't feel bad when you cut our way out of here."

A tiny figure skittered across the floor of their cell, jumping at Yevnir. It latched on to his thigh with an open mouth, and he screamed as he reached to tear it off.

Yevnir yanked and yanked, and finally the creature parted from his skin, leaving a little bite mark and a slow trickle of blood down his leg.

"Ow!" he yelped, snatching the creature in his hand. "Oh, it's you."

Sir Willam leaned down to catch a better glimpse of Yevnir's attacker. It was the tiger-striped squirrel. "That is the beast that led me to your house! I had never seen its like. Had you ever seen such a squirrel in Edra?"

"Squirrel?" replied Yevnir. "This is no squirrel, old friend. I take it it ate my letter?"

"Only a piece."

"Then my plan has worked."

"Your plan? This was your plan? You wanted to get me in a cell with you, with nothing but a useless squirrel to save us?"

"Shhh, she will hear you, and you found me, no?"

"Yes, and now we share the same cell."

"But you're here! And so is she. You want answers?" Yevnir held up the creature, which was trying to wiggle free in his hand. "This is where your answers lie. She is a squin, not a squirrel, and the reason you have never seen one before is because they don't exist anywhere else. They have never left the island, as far as I am aware.

"They are incredibly solitary creatures, you see, only found high in the mountains. Few have heard of the squin outside of Pastora, and fewer have heard of their powers. They have the remarkable ability of finding whatever they have a taste for. That is why when she ate my letter and tasted the drops of blood I infused in the parchment, she came looking for me. And that is why when I gave her a piece of gold early last year she led me to a tower on the Hollow Mountain and then to the buried treasure of our captors."

"So that's how you found your fortune? No schemes this time? Just a magical squirrel that eats everything but nuts?"

Yevnir smiled excitedly, revealing his chipped tooth. "Precisely."

Yevnir was an unusually comely man, with dark curly hair, brown eyes, and a complexion somewhere between Sir Willam's tan and the umber of the Ahkovans. He was notorious for his smile, the foundation upon which every successful lie he'd ever told had been built. Now, seeing that smile ruined by a chipped tooth and a swollen lip, Sir Willam couldn't help but feel sorry for his friend, despite knowing that every hardship Yevnir faced in his life had come to him of his own making, including this one.

Still, with all the room for sympathy in Sir Willam's heart, there was plenty left for contempt. "You've made a mess here, Yev, and for what? A bit of coin? Some treasure? A chalice here, a pearl necklace there? And where is it now? Where is your treasure?"

"I don't know."

Sir Willam nearly jumped.

"What? You don't know? You don't know! Damn you, Yevnir Goldleaf! They will kill us now. They will kill us both! The treasure was our only chance! You've doomed the both of us. And you're smiling. Happy now? You've finally killed me after all. You're finally the death of me. Was it worth it?"

Yevnir slumped back against the wall and stared up at the floorboards of the main deck, letting his arm rest against the floor without loosening his grip on the squin.

"Was it worth it?" he repeated. Yevnir's smirk turned into a grin, then his mouth opened to let out a chuckle, becoming an all-out roar of laughter.

That is it, Sir Willam thought. *I'm going to kill him.*

But as he watched Yevnir laugh, he remembered the playful young man he'd met in the tavern in Bordae, the young man who wanted to laugh at the world's expense, and he looked to the creature in his hands, attempting to gnaw on the fleshy part of his knuckle. A smile rose from the corners of his lips as it dawned on him.

"You don't know where your gold is because you knew you would tell them if you did."

Finally, Yevnir's laughter came to a gradual stop, and he reverted his gaze back to the knight. "You see it now, don't you?"

"I think I do. You hid the treasure somewhere and made sure, somehow, that you wouldn't be able to find it. That way if you were tortured you couldn't give it up because you truly don't know where it is. And the squin will help you find it when you're ready, as long as you give it more gold. But how did you know your blood on the letter would be enough to bring the thing back to you? What if the squin took a taste to the wax, the ink, or the parchment?"

"Plans work best when every step is well thought out, and up until now I must admit I had thought my plan was airtight. That detail was one of my most genius. I knew it would develop a taste for my blood rather than for the parchment or the other materials because I tested it. I used the same sort of parchment several times, each with a few drops of my blood on it. In every case, it went into a craze for the stuff. My blood. I thought about leaving a vial somewhere to make sure, but then of course it couldn't be guaranteed that you would find it."

"And why all the secrecy in your letter?"

"Because if the letter were to be intercepted, and it contained the whole truth, then they would know about the squin."

Sir Willam scratched his chin. "Did you train it to throw nuts at your window?"

"What? No. That would be ridiculous."

"It would not even make the list of the most absurd things you've done, Yev."

Yevnir scooted closer to get into the light, and pointing at the scar that ran across the palm of his free hand, he said, "I know none of this is ideal. I have sacrificed a lot." He stopped to sigh and rub his palm across his forehead. "You wouldn't ask if it was worth it if you saw this treasure. I assure you."

"So what went wrong? You said your plan is not as airtight as you had intended."

"You."

"Me?"

"Yes, you! You were supposed to find me and procure my escape. The squin led you right to me, but you were captured. Perhaps I was a fool to think you were the same knight who might have taken on the whole ship in his glory days."

"I am still in my glory days, you git. It is your fault I was captured. Your letter said to meet you at the inn, and you weren't there. I ran into Tessara instead, though I did make a mistake at your manor by letting her brother walk free."

"Ah, Varro, the first mate. Yes, you should've killed him. Lovely man, of course, soon-to-be father, but a pirate is a pirate."

"So what now?" Sir Willam asked.

"I am not done. Don't you want to know how I put my treasure in a place where even I could not find it?"

"I don't care. We need to give it back to the pirates so we can go free."

"Please let me tell you."

"Yev, I couldn't care less. Let's find a way out of here and get the treasure."

"I'll tell you anyway. Indulge me." Sir Willam sat down with an exasperated huff, and Yevnir continued, "This plan started forming long after I had found the treasure. When I arrived in Pastora over two years ago, I made the journey up the Hollow Mountain almost immediately. A local told me a story of the squins, and I had to find out if they were real. When I found one and discovered the legends of their gift to be true, I immediately began researching how to tame such a beast.

"It turns out that you cannot tame a squin. But you can use them if you know what you're doing. So I found the pirate treasure on the very beach you would have walked upon to get to this ship, and I built my home up in the mountain with a portion of the coin. It wasn't until I saw the Ahkovan pirates in the Hollow Mountain Inn that I knew I was in trouble. They were asking questions, trying to find out who had come away with their fortune, and it wouldn't be long until the locals mentioned my name. So, I took all the riches I had, including the gold and trinkets from that abandoned tower, and I gave them to a friend to hide them."

"You gave your entire fortune to a friend? But you've only been on the island for a few years. How did you know you could trust them? What if this friend were captured too?"

"That would be the day!" Yevnir chuckled. "To catch Arokis, they'd need much more than this little crew of scallywags. They'd need an army! And besides, he is impossible to find if he does not want to be found."

Sir Willam pushed into the iron bars at his back to sit up straight. "Who is Arokis?"

"*What* is Arokis? That is the question you should've asked. He is a giant, a very old giant, and a dear friend of mine."

"A giant?" The knight remembered the engraving he had seen in the abandoned tower, the one in which a giant shielded her face from a spear. What he had previously written off as fictitious folklore was beginning to seem more like a depiction of history. "Nothing should surprise me anymore, but a giant? That I would like to see. How do we find him?"

Yevnir raised his left hand in front of his face to show off the squin.

"We don't. We find the gold. Arokis will be sleeping. Probably for another month or so. Giants take long slumbers at this time of year. The only thing stopping us is this cell, but I'm formulating a plan as we speak. There is no reason to worry."

"Yes. I guess I'll take your word for it, then. It doesn't seem I have much of a choice."

"Don't be bitter, Will. I'm sorry about how things have

turned out. Truly, I am. But it is not as dire as it might seem now that we are together. Have I ever led you astray before?"

Sir Willam shut his eyes and leaned his head back against the cell door, contemplating the moment he decided to come rescue his friend. "Oh, never. Not even once." He made a silent promise that this would be the last time he would come to Yevnir's rescue, then wondered if he had made the same promise to himself all those years ago in Bordae.

CHAPTER SIX

"Will, did you hear that?"

"What is it?" Sir Willam sat up and turned his head. It had been hours since he'd been thrown in the cell.

"They've opened the hatch. I think she's coming down."

"Tessara?"

"Best to call her captain." Yevnir sat back and acted faint as the pirates approached.

Sir Willam turned his head to see three torches moving toward them. He shifted and pulled himself to his feet. "I'll do the talking, Yev."

"Knight." Tessara approached with Jakka and the other woman. Her mask was tied with a short string to her hip, so as she walked it bounced lightly against her upper thigh. "Have you found the gold?"

He froze, searching in vain for the right thing to say. "Uh . . ."

Tessara raised an eyebrow. On her right, Jakka stood grinning with murderous intent. The other woman looked eager, probably because her pay relied on the words Sir Willam failed to speak.

"I'm the only man on this island who can give you what you seek," Yevnir croaked defiantly. He stayed slumped against the back wall with his eyes closed and his head tilted so that it looked like he had no strength in his neck to keep it straight.

"So you were lying!" Tessara scolded. "You know the whole time. Good job, Sir Willam. The liar is broken. Now he will tell all."

"I'd rather die," Yevnir said. The knight knew this to be a lie. As much as Yevnir cherished gold, he valued nothing more than his own life.

"You both will die," Tessara said with a shrug. "Do you care if he dies?"

She pointed at Sir Willam, and he glared at Yevnir, thinking, *No, of course he doesn't, otherwise I would still be in Edra right now, at home in Horntree fishing with my brothers.*

"I do," Yevnir proclaimed. "I will show you where the treasure lies, if you spare him."

Now it was the knight's turn to raise an eyebrow. He knew Yevnir had no idea where the treasure was, but the lie was told with so much conviction that even Sir Willam wasn't sure what was true anymore. Would he actually lead them to the treasure? The squin—where had the squin gone? He searched the cell with his eyes and came up with nothing.

Wheeling around, he searched the spots of the hull that he could see in the scarce light. The squin had disappeared in the commotion.

Tessara gestured for Jakka to open the gate. The brute made eye contact with Sir Willam as he turned the key, daring him to try something. The door swung open and Jakka stepped through, shoved the knight back a step, then socked him in the jaw. Sir Willam's head spun, and he fell to one knee. His jaw throbbed where he had been hit, and he tasted metal on his tongue.

"Get up, donkey," said the brute.

The knight moved his jaw from side to side and then pushed himself to his feet. He got in Jakka's face, a few inches from butting heads with him. Jakka seemed surprised but also elated, like he'd been given an unexpected present. They stared at each other for just a moment before Sir Willam showed his teeth with a wide and playful smile.

"I believe my title is donkey *rider*."

Jakka hit him again, this time even harder, and sent him staggering back.

"Enough!" Tessara yelled. "Take us to our gold. You will come too, knight. Jakka, get rope and tie these two together. Ralle . . ." The other woman perked up to heed her captain's orders. "Ready the crew. We go to our treasure now. All of us."

Ralle went off to do as she was bid while Jakka and Tessara used their free hands to drag the two Edrans from their cell. After a struggle to get Yevnir to his feet, Tessara shoved him forward and prodded him along to the front, and they trudged through the dark hull and up the ladder to the main deck. Climbing the ladder was a challenge with bound hands, but a slew of pirates pulled Yevnir up onto the deck and then Sir Willam after Tessara had already gone up.

They stood there on the deck, the liar and the knight, shivering in the cold air that rolled in on the Callaseen tide. Surrounded by pirates. Hands bound. Their lives depended on how well Yevnir could lie. *I am in good hands now*, Sir Willam thought, the pirates bustling and grouping around them. *I will see Edra again.*

Yevnir snuck a glance at him. "'Donkey rider,' Will?" he said under his breath. "Are you trying to get us killed? Stop antagonizing the pirates."

"Don't tell me how to navigate your mess!" he whispered back.

"We're not going to get out of this by force. That plan is out the window now. You need to listen to me. Placate and pander. Placate and pander. Do you understand?"

Sir Willam clenched his fists.

"Those weapons are not in my arsenal, Yev."

Yevnir looked him up and down, nodding at the blood trickling from his nose. "Clearly."

"Ready the boats!" Tessara barked. She moved swiftly to Yevnir's ear, and he straightened as she whispered, "Take us to our gold, liar."

Two huge men picked him up like he was a basket of flowers. They carried him, kicking and thrashing in their arms, to a rowboat suspended by ropes. As it lowered, they threw him in and jumped in after.

Sir Willam glanced back at Jakka. "You will handle me with more care than that, surely? I'm a knight, you know. You shouldn't throw knights. We are vengeful creatures, really, with lots of friends."

Jakka grimaced. "Where are your friends?" He threw Sir Willam over his shoulder, just as he had coming down the mountain. Soon Sir Willam was in a boat too, cutting the short distance between the ship and the shore.

The waves sent spouts of water over the sides of their rowboat, dousing his cloak. He shivered and looked up at Jakka, who stared at him from the front of the boat as the other pirates rowed. Jakka crinkled his nose, and Sir Willam could've sworn he heard his thoughts—murderous, evil thoughts. When they hit land, a few more rowboats came in right beside them. It was most of the ship's crew. Varro had been left behind.

The crew on the beach began lighting torches, pulling their rowboats farther inland and taking what they needed for the journey. The knight watched them with a pitiful kind of amusement. He knew what it was like to blindly follow Yevnir's directions and have no other choice but to do so. They were stuck, as he was stuck when he'd first received the letter weeks before. Without him, there was no treasure, so the pirates had no other choice but to follow his word, but for Sir Willam the predicament was much more personal.

When the letter came to him, he was stuck because he was not the kind of person who could ignore a friend in need, and he was angry because he knew that part of him was being exploited.

"Lead the way." Tessara gestured for Yevnir to start walking. Immediately the two brutes who had thrown him into the boat came up on either side of him. Sir Willam was in the front of the group with Yevnir, Tessara, Jakka, and the two brutes, a trail of pirates behind them.

"Where are we going?" asked Tessara playfully, her serious captain voice left behind on the rough ocean waves.

"A castle," said Yevnir. "Arduny Castle. Have you heard of it?"

"It's not my first time on the island, liar. I know Arduny Castle. It's a fortress. Why there?"

"I am friends with the Barnum family," he replied. "Lord Barnum was an old gambling acquaintance of mine, even before I came to Pastora when his father was still lord of Arduny. It's a funny story actually, how we met—"

"You are friends with Barnum, not me," Tessara interrupted. "How do I know you are not leading us to a trap?" They kept moving as they talked, approaching the edge of a forest. "They will see we are pirates and arrest us."

"Not if I tell them you are with me," Yevnir replied.

"You could let them take us. You could trick us. Why not do this?"

"Because your sword will be closer to me than theirs will be to any of you. If I betray you, you can stab me in the back."

Tessara shared an uneasy glance with Ralle then huffed and focused her attention ahead instead of on Yevnir. In the end, her questions and her reluctance would do her little good. If she wanted her gold, she was at the will of Yevnir. The Ahkovan pirates were now all depending on and subjugated by the word of a liar. *That is his genius*, Sir Willam thought, watching Tessara stomp ahead in front of the group, rendered powerless by a man much smaller and weaker than herself. *He can bring kings to their knees to bow, and he can turn outlaws, who live to break the rules, into servants of his will. That is much more powerful than the dinky piece of metal I swing around.*

...

It was morning now. They had walked through the night, stopping only to fetch water and rest their legs. Sir Willam could've done without the short breaks, which seemed to thaw out his legs from their numb state and make it twice as hard to continue when they started up again. His only solace was the vocal complaints of the rest of the crew, and especially Yevnir's constant cries for a break and a nap.

The knight's head lulled and bobbed like Captain Tarrick's ship coming into harbor. Each step he fought sleep, but he knew if *he* was struggling, then Yevnir was in agony. The Bordaen had never been much for adversity.

The sun rose and snuck its golden beams through the leaves, and the squirrels scuttled across branches, squeaking and cracking their breakfast nuts, while the birds woke with their early morning songs. Sir Willam Hornsby thought of nothing but home.

He remembered early mornings in his village as a child, getting up to fish with his brothers before the sun had risen. He remembered trekking through the forest, his boots collecting moisture on the way to their favorite pond, and suddenly he was there. They waded through the tall grass together. It felt so real, like a memory playing out in the present.

His brother Philip smiled back at him. His blue eyes and brown hair were similar to Willam's, but they seemed so foreign to him now. His big brother took off running, and Willam chased him until they reached the edge of the pond. A light wave of fog hovered over the water's surface, and the sun peeked through the trees with a dull orange light, not quite ready to shine in its full glory.

His head lolled, and his eyes opened to see a pirate. Jakka's giant frame bounced with every step. "Don't steal this from me, brute." Jakka's body morphed, and he became his brother Philip again.

Philip slipped off his boots and set them neatly by the tall grass. Willam flicked his off and tossed them to the side. He plopped down at the edge, at a little overhang high enough for a young boy to dangle his feet from. When his toes touched the water, they sent a ripple out into the stagnant pond. His foot sank up to the ankle with a small splash that broke the ripple. He could feel it, the cold on his feet, the movement of the water until it went still again, his big brother by his side.

He smiled, closed his eyes, and breathed in the dewy morning air. He was happy to be home, wondering about what his other brothers were up to. When he opened his eyes, Philip was staring at him, his lips moved and his mouth opened, but it was not his voice that spoke.

"We're here."

Sir Willam's head shot up, unsure whose voice he'd heard. How he had continued to walk in such a vivid dream he had no idea, but it was true. They had arrived at Arduny Castle. They stood at the forest edge, looking on to a valley of flat land. There were long fields of wheat and corn, and little cottages with grass roofs like the ones he'd seen in Biverna. A dirt road led from the mountain pass to the east, up to the castle's two-towered gatehouse. The portcullis was of thick black metal, like it was made from an anchor, but the castle itself was white as marble.

From their position, Willam could see the first of the curtain walls that wrapped around to the river behind the castle. The river flowed in the shadow of the great keep at the northernmost point of the fortress. It was an impressive keep, with several turrets and towers, many of which had green and gold banners that hung down half their height, displaying the sigil of house Barnum, a mountain goat with gold horns.

The eastern side of the castle was all that was touched by the sun's light, making it look like those parts of the castle were made of golden bricks. But in all the glamor of their view from the tree line, Sir Willam's favorite sight was the shine on the river, the glimmer and the sparkle of water rushing in the light of the sun then going dark in the castle's shadow.

There was a short section of the river, between the sparkle and the shadow, where the water glowed with a dull orange, like the pond beyond the tall grass. Willam knew in this moment what Yevnir had meant in his letter when he wrote, "I'm afraid I'll never see the dawn again." He hadn't meant the next morning of his life in Pastora. He hadn't even meant that he was scared to die, although he undoubtedly was. When Yev said "dawn," he meant Edra. He meant home.

Suddenly growing fearful, for a moment he no longer cared for his reputation or his honor. Being a knight didn't matter. Being a good friend meant nothing. All that mattered was the pond beyond the tall grass. All that mattered was seeing his brothers again—Philip, Sampson, and John. It was a horrible feeling that made his stomach turn and his throat tighten. These values he held on to so dearly suddenly felt secondary to his survival when they never had before. It wasn't as if this was the first time his life had been threatened, though perhaps it wasn't the thought of dying alone that scared him but the thought of dying so far from home.

All he knew was that whatever happened in this castle, he was going to survive it, if for nothing else than to go fishing with his brothers one more time.

Before the group continued toward the castle, Tessara had an announcement to make, "If the Edrans try to trick us here, kill them both."

CHAPTER SEVEN

Sir Willam looked to Yevnir, whose face displayed nothing but confidence, even under threat of death. *This better work*, he thought. *I don't want to die for you.*

They walked through the valley and past the farms—a pirate crew thirty strong from the isle of Ahkova, and a liar and a knight from Edra. Lord Barnum's subjects turned their heads from harvesting their crops, gripped scythe or pitchfork, and watched the procession approach the gate.

Before they could reach the gatehouse, they heard a "Halt!" from the battlements. Sir Willam looked up to see a row of archers with their bowstrings pulled back to their ears. The pirates rushed together in a sort of haphazard formation. It was a useless tactic, seeing as none of them had shields, but it was more of a reflexive reaction than a defensive position. Jakka stepped in front of his captain, tightening his muscled chest as if it could deflect any arrow that came for her.

"Tell them!" Tessara snapped.

Yevnir gestured for her to cut the rope that bound his hands then said, "If Lord Barnum sees I am your prisoner, he will have you all killed. He is very fond of me."

Tessara reluctantly cut the rope, giving him a look through her painted mask and a shake of her dagger before he stepped forward from the group.

"Come no farther!" shouted a guard from a slit in the wall below the battlements. The tip of this guard's arrow pointed through the slit, aimed directly at Yevnir's chest.

Yevnir put his hands up. "We come in peace, friend. I am the Edran, Yevnir Goldleaf of Bordae. Your master will know the name. Bring him to the walls and tell him Yevnir has come to speak about the gold."

"You are *the* Goldleaf?" asked a different guard from the battlements.

"Yes, I am!" he replied with a large grin. "The famous Goldleaf." He turned to wink at Sir Willam.

"Get the lord!" someone shouted. "Hurry!"

Yevnir walked back toward the pirates. "You see," he said, folding his arms, "there is no trick. This was all a misunderstanding. It's as I told you from the beginning. I didn't know the gold was yours when I found it. No man in their right mind would steal from Captain Tessara."

She glared at him, some loose strands of her braided hair catching the slight breeze.

"Why put it here?" asked the captain. "You fear we come looking?"

"You *feared* we would. You're talking about the past," Sir Willam said, immediately noticing the hateful stares of the pirates. "So that's . . . how you would say it. My apologies." He stared at the ground to avoid their gaze.

Yevnir butted in to save him, "I put it here for safekeeping, yes, but not from you. I mean, from pirates in general, of course. Stealing gold *is* what pirates do, and you are not the only pirates who like to land in Pastora. The bay on the south of the island is called the Bay of Pirates for a reason. But soon you will have your gold back, worry not."

"GOLDLEAF!"

The pirates jerked their heads up to follow the voice, but Yevnir kept his back turned, flinching at the noise and keeping his shoulders and neck shrugged. Sir Willam caught his eye.

"That's you, Yev," he whispered.

"Does he look angry?"

Sir Willam looked up at where the voice had come from. A large broad-shouldered man stood with his arms on both sides of a crenel. His face, which was already adorned with a bushy reddish-orange beard, was made redder by his flushed scowl and crunched nose. He wore a dark-green robe with gold lining, and his fingers which were clenched into fists pressed against the stone of the battlements, held several bejeweled rings.

Sir Willam looked back at his friend. "I wouldn't say he looks delighted to see you, no."

Yevnir cringed and forced himself to turn.

"Lord Barnum!" he shouted with false but rather convincing enthusiasm.

The lord huffed and looked down into the castle courtyard. "Open the bloody gates!"

As the portcullis lifted, the crew cautiously passed beneath it. They arrived in a square courtyard surrounded by walls. Ahead, a large wooden door stood between them and the rest of the castle. The sounds of armor clanging and swords flying from their scabbards were the first things they heard, and suddenly they were surrounded. Spears and halberds boxed them in. Fully armored knights with their swords drawn and castle guards with chainmail and iron half helms flooded in between them and the exit.

The Ahkovans drew their scimitars. Sir Willam reached for his sword reflexively, even though he knew one of the pirates had his belongings. Tessara swept behind Yevnir and pressed her dagger against his throat.

"Lower your weapons," she shouted to Lord Barnum's men, "or I kill him."

Lord Barnum climbed down the steps from the battlements.

"Good," he said as he descended, "you will be saving me the trouble. But if he hasn't told you where he's put my Violet's bracelet, then it will be you who dies next."

"Bracelet?" Tessara hissed in Yevnir's ear, pressing the knife tighter so that it broke the skin.

Yevnir choked. "I . . . I have no idea what he's talking about."

"You said he was a friend," said the captain.

"Did I? I thought I said acquaintance."

Sir Willam butted in, "Why would he lead himself into a trap? The lord wants to kill him too!"

Tessara glared at the knight, loosened her grip on the knife, and pushed Yevnir away.

"You," said Lord Barnum, "are you the Edran knight I heard rumors of? The one asking questions? Yes, the Bivernian described you well. What is your business in this?"

"Goldleaf is a friend, my lord. I came to Pastora to save him from the pirates. Well, I didn't know originally what I had come to save him from. But I came to save him."

"You seem to be doing a swell job of it," the lord mocked, gesturing toward the pirates and his own men. "You say you don't know what you've come to save him from. Then I will tell you. You've come to save him from himself. His greed. Your friend, the Goldleaf, tricked my fool of a son into gambling away the most expensive piece of jewelry on the entire island. It was his mother's, my Violet. A golden bracelet with rubies. But the gold was the rare bit. Boncopan gold. I'm sure you've heard of its value. So you understand now why you have come to save him and why he cannot be saved."

"We can help," Tessara suggested desperately. "Give us our treasure, and we make him find your bracelet."

Sir Willam shook his head, shocked at the captain's wishful

thinking. "He doesn't have your treasure, my lady," he said aloud. She looked at him, confused.

"That I don't," said Lord Barnum. "I don't know what you're looking for, but I don't have it. To find my own treasure, however, I must have Yevnir alive, which means I'll be taking him from your custody, pirate. Unless you know where the bracelet is. Then I will kill him and spare you. Otherwise, my men will be taking you to the cells."

"You lied!" Tessara snapped her head toward Yevnir, who had been slowly inching away from her as she and the lord were talking. Her eyes filled with rage. She ripped her scimitar from her belt and charged him. Sir Willam dove between Jakka and Ralle, barreling into Tessara.

Her scimitar flew from her hand and clattered to the ground. She reached for it, but a swarm of castle guards was on her, wrenching her to her feet then dragging her away. A volley of arrows flew into the crowd of pirates, killing a few and injuring many more.

The spears and halberds jutted forward. Jakka slashed three spears away and charged in between them. An arrow found his back, but he kept slashing wildly. He killed two spearmen and knocked another unconscious on his back swing before a sword found his belly and a spear pierced his side. He looked around incredulously, blood spewing from his wounds, in disbelief at his own mortality, then he closed his eyes forever.

The pirates had laid down their weapons before Jakka had even fallen. They were surrounded and outnumbered three to one. Sir Willam freed his hands with Tessara's scimitar then grabbed Yevnir and dragged him away from the pirates. Lord Barnum's guards let them through the thick wooden door into the rest of the castle, leaving the Ahkovan crew behind in the courtyard. They were accompanied by four knights with their swords drawn and ready.

From the corner of his eye, through the gaps between the

knights around him, he saw Tessara kicking and screaming as they dragged her to the dungeons. Her mask had flown off, her long braids thrashing wildly about her face as they came loose from the tie that was holding them. *She will give them hell,* thought Sir Willam.

In the keep, they were forced through a narrow hall and down a steep flight of stairs until they came into a room with a large open terrace looking out on to the river. Lord Barnum was waiting for them there, smirking as they approached. "I had been looking for you, you know," the lord said. "I had my men out searching for weeks after you took the bracelet."

"Won. I won the bracelet, my lord."

"Either way, you are here now. Delivered by pirates, of all people."

As the lord walked closer, the guards fell behind Yevnir and Sir Willam, so that they were standing alone with Lord Barnum.

Yevnir smiled, and the lord smiled back. Yev raised his arms as if for a hug. Sir Willam looked back and forth between them. *Wait,* he thought, *has the lord been in on this the whole time? Are they really friends?* Lord Barnum swung his fist so hard it knocked Yevnir flat on his back. Sir Willam watched him fall. *Nope.*

Yevnir got up, holding his nose as the blood came rushing. "Wait," he pleaded, "I can get your bracelet. My friend is bringing it here as we speak!"

"Your friend?" Lord Barnum scoffed. "I was your friend once! I was amazed to learn this knight here was your friend. You think I would so easily believe you have another?"

"You can see with your own eyes." Yevnir turned his head slightly to make it clear what he was looking at.

Lord Barnum frowned, gave his guards a threatening look, then turned. His green robe swirled after him as his broad shoulders whipped around, and he saw it at the same time as

Sir Willam, his movement revealing what his body had previously blocked. It was the squin.

Perched on the sill of the large open window with the view of the river behind her, she held a shining gold and ruby bracelet in front of her chest by both mouth and paws.

Sir Willam looked at Yevnir, who, ever proud of reaching the latest goal mark in his plan, sported an outrageously smug grin. "How in the name of—"

"Goldleaf!" yelled the lord. The belly laugh that followed was the only difference from the first time he'd yelled the name that day. Barnum swung back around, his arms held out wide and with a grin on his face to rival Yevnir's.

The switch from wanting to kill a man to looking like he was going to hug him was alarming. Sir Willam was now not only impressed by Yevnir's timing but also his courage to take from a man who could turn so quickly. The knight had dealt with a lot of lords in his lifetime, whether working for or against them, and he knew the ones who could switch their demeanor like this in the blink of an eye were the most dangerous.

"You have no idea how happy this will make my Violet," said the lord. "And you've brought me a squin to boot! How did you tame such a creature? No, that is not the question. How did you hear of it? Those who grow up on the island hear of them from our mothers and our nursemaids. You are an outsider, a foreigner." The lord laughed heartily, glancing back and forth between Yevnir and the squin. "Bugger all that. Well done!" Turning to the squin, he went down to a knee and said, "Come here, little tiger."

She glanced back and forth, her beady yellow eyes darting from Yevnir to Lord Barnum. "Go on," Yevnir encouraged. The squin scurried over to the lord and tentatively dropped the bracelet at his feet. As soon as it fell from her mouth, she bolted to where Yevnir stood and shot up his leg. In a second, she was resting on his shoulder. She shuffled toward his neck and put her paws on top of his ear, using it to shield her eyes from the scary red-haired lord, who had begun cradling the golden bracelet like a newborn child.

Yevnir stepped forward. "Unfortunately, my lord, I cannot give you my squin as a gift. She has taken to me and would not serve anyone else." Sir Willam knew this to be a lie. Only a day ago the thing had been latched on to Yevnir's leg and trying to drink his blood. "However, she has been very good to me, and if you secure my freedom, she can be very good to you as well."

The lord's joy vanished as quickly as it had come. His fists clenched again, and his cheeks reddened.

"Get to it, Goldleaf. I have already grown sick of your yammering."

"It is true, what your mother and your nursemaid told you about the creatures, and I have a mountain of gold to prove it. If you free me and my companion, a third of that treasure will be yours."

Now Sir Willam interjected, "Will you not let us go, my lord? He has brought you your bracelet."

"Of course he won't, Will! I still have a debt to settle with him. Lord Barnum deserves more than a bracelet that was rightfully his in the first place."

The lord scoffed. "Don't try to honey me, deceiver. If I let you go, how will I know you'll make good on this arrangement?"

Yevnir looked around, perhaps surprised that his attempt at flattery wasn't enough to free them. His eyes settled on Sir Willam, and he patted him once hard on the back.

"You can keep the knight as assurance until I'm back!"

"No, you cannot!" he argued. "Yev, what are you doing?" The two friends turned to face each other, the squin now relaxing instead of hiding on Yevnir's shoulder, although she kept her eyes fixed on the lord.

"I will be back," Yevnir explained. "I wouldn't leave you to die. How could I when you've come all this way to save me?"

Sir Willam squinted and thought to himself, *Because you are a self-absorbed git*, but he said nothing aloud.

"Your friend doesn't trust that you will come back with the gold, so why should I?" Lord Barnum looked at his guards again. This time they readied their spears at Yevnir's and Sir Willam's backs.

"Because, my lord, he is a treasure in his own right."

The lord raised an eyebrow, equally intrigued and suspicious.

"Have you not heard of the legendary Sir Willam Hornsby?" continued Yevnir. "The slayer of the Bordaen Sceuorg? The liberator of Dunford Abbey? The champion of . . ."

"Never heard of him."

"Right. If you were from Edra, you would have. Every man, woman, and child knows the name, and he is beloved by the lords of Edra. Any number of them would pay a hefty price to know he was safe. The king himself would go to great lengths to save him. So I can bring you back your share of the loot, a fortune's worth, or you can make your fortune off his ransom. Your choice."

"Is this true, knight? Are you Sir Willam Hornsby, the slayer of the whatever and liberator of who knows where? Beloved by Edran nobility? Upon your honor, you will answer me true." There was something in the way Lord Barnum said this that made the knight uneasy. His tone dared him to lie, hoped for it even, like how Jakka had left his hands free so he might try to escape.

"It is true, my lord," Sir Willam replied. But was it? Had he forsaken his honor with this lie? Or was he telling it true? He had done all of those things, earned all of those titles, but he wasn't sure the lords loved him for it. The common folk adored him, but the lords of Edra—and King Gramon, most of all—

loved blood far more than deeds, and his was as noble as the orphan boy Ardee, whom he'd met in Biverna.

"Then it is settled," Lord Barnum declared. "Yevnir Goldleaf will leave Arduny Castle immediately, accompanied by my guards, of course, and bring me back one third of his treasure. If he fails to—"

"Wait! No, no, that won't do. I must go alone."

"Alone?" Lord Barnum snorted. "Alone?" He looked at his guards, who, despite their attempts at stoicism, were taken over by bouts of laughter. "Do you hear this Edran weasel? You'll be alone in the grave, Goldleaf! You'll have cheated and schemed away any companions you might've had by then. For now, you will go with a team of my best men. They will watch you every second and kill you at any misstep."

"Come off it, Yevnir!" shouted Sir Willam. "For once, stick to a plan. No tricks. I want to go home."

"No, I'm afraid that cannot happen. It is for loyalty to a friend that I cannot allow it. The deal is off."

Before the lord's rage could boil and spill over the top, scolding everyone near him, Sir Willam threw out a risky request. "My lord, could I have a moment with my friend? We need to discuss this."

Lord Barnum threw his hand up and rolled his eyes then fell back to the table behind him and took a seat. Willam grabbed his friend by the shoulder, making the squin flinch and duck behind his ear. A gilded tapestry hung on the wall beside them, depicting a battle in magnificent color but of little significance to the two Edrans who huddled beside it.

Sir Willam whispered so that just the two of them could hear, "What are you thinking, Yev? It's time you clued me in. If this is some ploy, I think you've really miscalculated."

"It's no ploy. It's Arokis. He does not like the Barnums, and if I were seen retrieving the treasure he hid for me, with a group of Barnum's men, well, he might not be so friendly anymore."

"I thought you said Arokis was asleep."

"Arokis is asleep, but the other beasts of this island are not. If they see me with men from Arduny, they will wake him, and he won't wait for me to explain my side. We will all be dead far before that. Besides, he is my friend, and I wouldn't side with his enemy."

Sir Willam scowled.

"Stop acting as if you're a loyal friend. You are not. You were ready to do this until he insisted on sending his men with you. You don't care about loyalty. Don't pretend to. Not with me." The two of them looked over to Lord Barnum, realizing Sir Willam had just raised his voice in anger.

The lord stared back and gestured for them to continue. Willam sighed and leaned against the tapestry. "Why does Arokis dislike the Barnums?" His tone softened slightly, and he was back to a whisper.

"They killed his mother, a thousand years ago—chased her down. She took out many of his men before she finally fell, but fell she did, and he has hated them ever since."

"Is that what I saw in the treasury of that tower on the mountain? Was it Barnum's soldiers chasing the creatures into the woods?"

"I don't know what you're talking about. No, it wouldn't be. That tower is far older than a thousand years. It was probably a depiction of the Epulites."

"The what?"

"It's a Sydian thing, you pagan," Yevnir joked. "It's one of our stories. You wouldn't know it."

"No, I wouldn't," he replied coldly. "So how are we to get out of this?"

Yevnir stared up at the tapestry then down at his feet. A few moments passed like that, and Sir Willam began to get nervous. He could feel the guards eyeing them, and he imagined Lord Barnum was making a list in his head of the most gruesome ways to put them both to death. Finally, Yevnir stroked the squin's head gently with two fingers and stepped back to the center of the room.

Lord Barnum stood. "Are you ready then to continue as planned?"

"Not quite as planned, no. But with a new plan," said Yevnir. "Sir Willam here, accompanied by the squin, will go retrieve your treasure. They will leave here *alone*. He will gather men in Biverna to help him. I will give him suggestions before he leaves. But he will *not* be accompanied by your men. This would prove to be dangerous for all of us for reasons I cannot discuss. When he brings back your share of the treasure, then we will all go our separate ways. How does that sound?"

The room was silent. Sir Willam braced himself for the switch in Lord Barnum's countenance that would mean their deaths. Instead, the lord spoke calmly, "You insult me. I don't know how to respond. First you tell me he is insurance, and now you want to take his place."

"You know I only chose this route because I am confident he will come back. He is a knight, after all, and his honor would be at stake in this endeavor. I am a selfish man. A greedy one. Everybody knows this. But Sir Willam is loyal and would not leave me to die. Nor would he betray his word. All of Edra could attest to that. The pirates in your cells would even have to admit that the man is loyal to a fault. This is the only viable option, my lord."

"I do not know Sir Willam Hornsby. I see him in front of me, so you say, but I do not know of his name, nor am I aware of his exploits. Why should I trust that he is the man you say he is? Why should I trust that the man you say he is even exists? I had never heard of this knight, whom you claim is famous and beloved. He could be a common man, for all I know, wrapped in a knight's cloak and trained to play the part."

Lord Barnum hadn't seemed to snap; if anything, he seemed calmer now. Perhaps Sir Willam had misjudged him.

"My lord . . ." A voice came from behind Yevnir and Sir Willam, one of the guards. He straightened his body, put his spear to his side, and bowed his head slightly. "May I speak, my lord?"

"Go on."

"I have heard of Sir Willam Hornsby, slayer of the Bordaen Sceuorg and liberator of Dunford Abbey. My cousin was a monk at Dunford. He wrote to me often, before the abbey was taken over by the Morridans and . . . well . . . whatever else was there, then he didn't. For a year he didn't write me. I figured him dead. The week after they were liberated, I received a letter. He described the torture and the agony he had been through, then he praised his liberator, Sir Willam Hornsby."

"Yes," said the lord, "that is very touching. What a great story. However, we do not know if this is him."

"My lord . . . my cousin Teneir described the knight as wearing a black cloak with a tree-shaped bronze brooch."

Sir Willam smiled. Good deeds did pay off, it seemed. This was a first.

Lord Barnum looked Sir Willam up and down, seeing the cloak and the bronze brooch. "Very well. Bring me the gold, Sir Willam Hornsby, or your friend dies . . ."

CHAPTER EIGHT

Sir Willam pulled hard on the paddles of his rowboat, leaning back for momentum and then forward again as he lifted and plopped the paddles back in the water for another pull. Over and over again, he repeated this motion, watching the white towers of Arduny Castle and the fertile fields beyond it disappear behind a range of mountains.

In the pocket of his cloak was one gold coin given to him by Yevnir right before he took off. He had instructions to toss it to the squin when—and only when—he was ready to find the treasure. It was an ancient coin, which Yevnir had found in the old tower Sir Willam had discovered the engraving in, and Yevnir was adamant that there would be no others on the island with the same taste, other than in his cache of treasure.

The squin sat across from him on the other bench, watching him heave and sweat. She stared at him for a while, as if she wanted to help, then curled up and nodded off to sleep. For hours he rowed, never noticing his arms tiring or his back aching. There were more important things on his mind than aches and pains—finding a crew, for one.

Along with the coin, Yevnir had given him a list, a very

peculiar list, of people who might agree to the task. Although his friend had seemed confident they would all join, Sir Willam was less so. If Yevnir were with him, it would be one thing, but the knight had never credited himself with having any gift of persuasion, and having to do it alone seemed an impossible task.

The knight rowed into a shadow. The sun was at its peak in the sky, but still a mountain shrouded its light. He turned in his boat. Ahead of him stood the Hollow Mountain, enormous and green as ever. *It is nothing against you, dear mountain,* he thought, *but I hope I never see you again after this.*

Forest carpeted the base of the mountain all the way to the riverbank. In the highest spots, the river had eroded away the bank and revealed the roots of the trees so that they looked like decaying men whose rib cages had been exposed. Even in the low spots, where there were small dirt beaches riddled with driftwood and fallen birch, a fisherman's discarded rope here and there, the trees seemed to lean over the water and add to the shadow the mountain already cast over the whole section of the river in which he rowed.

The point was quickly approaching where he was meant to land. Not far down from there, the river bent and flowed west. A fish jumped and shook off its scales in midair before returning to the water with a huge splash that made the squin jump and peek over the side of the boat.

Sir Willam watched the fish yearningly. As large rings rippled through the water from where it landed, the knight let out a sigh and looked down to the floor of his boat. A pile of fishing nets teased him below the seat the squin sat upon, and old scales and blood stains on the wood begged him to go after that jumping fish. A drop of rain hit his neck and ruined his daydream, then another, and then he was caught in the nightmare of a heavy downpour.

His boat hit land, and he hurried out of it, pulling his hood over his head and his cloak tight around his neck. He dragged the rowboat far enough onto the bank that he could tie it off to a boulder then grabbed his sword belt from the bench, which Lord Barnum had allowed him to take after no small amount of negotiating.

The rain quickly became cold and unforgiving, coming in from the west along with a powerful wind. The river seemed to disappear in a haze of mist. Sir Willam turned to run into the forest at the foot of the mountain, eager for the cover. What stopped him was a desperate squeal. A terrified whimper.

"Oh, don't play the helpless maiden!" he shouted through the rain. The whimper came again. Jumping back into the boat, which rocked with the wind and had already begun to fill with rainwater, he fumbled around for the creature. "Where are you?" Lightning cracked overhead, followed by a deafening roar of thunder. "Squin!" he shouted. The rain was too loud now to hear the squin's pleas for help.

Hands rummaging through the water, throwing away bits of rope and empty sacks, Sir Willam began to panic. His breath quickened until he was panting. The aches he had refused to feel earlier came stabbing back all at once. He forced his hand up over his face to block the wind and made one last push to find her. Even in his fight against the rain and the rising water in his boat, he could feel the heaviness of his eyelids from his lack of sleep.

His boots sloshed through the water. His feet had never felt so heavy. He yelled out in frustration. Lightning struck over the mountainside, and there she was floating lifelessly, her left foot caught in a net. He grabbed her. "No . . . NO!" She was his only chance of finding the treasure, of saving Yevnir from Lord Barnum's wrath. And she was gone.

He crouched in the middle of the boat, the squin in his hands, huddled up in a ball of defeat. The water rose rapidly, now reaching up to his knees. The rain pelted his cloak. He was content to let it be, to let the river swallow him and to let his mission fail. Yevnir would never forgive him. Then again, Yevnir would die before he had the chance to hold a grudge. As for the treasure, it would be lost, perhaps until the giant Arokis woke up, if he even remembered where he'd hid it after a few months' sleep.

The idea of fishing with his brothers now seemed a fool's dream. Even if he made it home, would his brothers ever forgive him for pursuing this life? For leaving them? He sat down in the water that had filled his boat, leaning his back against the bench. His hands hovered in front of him, holding the squin's body above the surface of the water.

"I'm sorry, little squin. This is no way to die. I wish Yevnir had left you with your family up on the mountain. He has a way of roping others into things. Now we'll both die for his greed."

He began to chuckle. "Nagri Attun," he said. "How fitting." The phrase meant something like "nature's grace." It referred to the inevitability of death, of nature allowing you a break from the struggle of life. Light streaked through the dark-gray sky. Thunder boomed. "Oh hush, now!" he screamed, staring up at it. "Let me die in peace."

He closed his eyes and let the rain fall on his face. It was over. If the squin was dead, then so was Yevnir, and if he could not save his friend, then in his mind he was not worthy of leaving this island. There was a peacefulness to this surrender. He would have to save no one else, slay no other beast. It was the end.

Suddenly he felt something. A thump. The softest yet most significant little beat. He sat up, water falling down his chest. He brought the squin close and prodded her with a finger. She was alive. Or at least her heart was still beating. Faintly, weakly, but beating. "Alright, squin. Don't die. Please don't die! We're not giving up."

He wrapped her in one hand and squeezed. Her tiny neck jerked back, but she went limp. He squeezed again. Nothing.

Taking her gently into both hands, he brought her little face to his mouth and blew softly then squeezed again. Her neck jerked back and this time stayed back, tension returning to her muscles. Her eyes bulged from her head and she coughed. He set her on the bench, which was barely above the water. She stood shakily on her little paws, and Sir Willam tapped her back lightly with a finger. The squin coughed and spat until finally she stood straight, all the water purged from her lungs. She shook the water from her coat, even as the rain replaced it, and let out a whimpering cry.

"Ha, ha!" Sir Willam jumped with excitement. He scooped the squin up into his arms and spun around in the boat, splashing and almost tripping in the knee-high water. "Let's go find that gold! Then we can both go home. How does that sound?"

He opened his collar and let her nuzzle in his cloak and leather jerkin. Together they got out of the boat, and Sir Willam ran toward the wood line to get out of the rain. He plopped down under a tree and brought his cloak over his head. It was soaking wet, so it didn't bring the comfort he'd expected, but he relished the moment nonetheless. Under this soaked and sagging cloak he held the squin in both hands and smiled, utterly relieved.

"Thank you for not giving up on me, my friend." He had no light to see her reaction and no reason to believe she would have one, but he imagined her smiling back at him.

An hour later, the rain had stopped, the sun had returned to the sky, and the squin had returned to her wild, lively nature. Sir Willam walked through the forest, squishing and slipping in the mud, with the squin on his shoulder. She seemed to bask in the sun everywhere it came through the trees. She pranced on Sir Willam's shoulder and hopped on a branch only to hop right back, reveling in a life she'd almost lost.

Biverna was but a mile away. Once they turned the corner, there it would be. Although relieved for the squin's revival, Sir Willam felt he had been so ready to give up, to let Yevnir die. It was easy to sit down and never get up, to let the world swallow him whole and leave his troubles behind. But he was a knight, and he'd never succumbed to ease before. Something about this land had changed him. He'd become selfish and weak.

As they approached the end of the forest and the town of Biverna, he thought to himself, *I will have to be the old me if I'm to finish this, the Sir Willam from the stories.*

The knight had mixed feelings when he saw the outline of Biverna peeking through the trees ahead. On the one hand, he felt excited. He had made it, and they were one step closer to getting the gold. On the other, he was terrified he would fall short. He couldn't believe it. It had been so long since he'd truly felt afraid. He was alive—not alive to carry out his duties and free Yevnir, but alive for himself. He wanted to *live* to see Horntree again, and suddenly this quest felt like more than just his reluctant duty. This fear was rejuvenating.

Sir Willam would still have to find a crew, purchase some mules on the credit of some to-be-retrieved hidden treasure, and of course actually find said treasure. These conflicting feelings were both pushed down and numbed so that he could only hear their distant cries for attention, and all by uttering the same phrase to himself.

"You are the Sir Willam from the stories."

Every step he took, he repeated it silently in his head, until, opening the door to the Hollow Mountain Inn, he had forgotten the meaning of the word anxiety—a word which, even yesterday, aboard the *Loyal Blue*, he never would have thought would apply to him.

He paid no attention to the curious stares of the men at the booths or the sly looks of the women dancing around him. He was well aware of the condition he was in. His face was bruised and swollen, his lip was split, and he was dripping puddles onto the floor from his cloak.

Not to mention there was a mythical creature riding on his shoulder. They would have to get used to all of that, but he needed a drink.

The inn had a completely different ambiance from the last time he'd been in it. Instead of loud music and cheerful dancing, there was a slower, more somber melody that only women were dancing to. A different bard and a different band played in the back-right corner of the room, their lyrics in a language he couldn't understand. He didn't care enough at the moment to ask himself why only women were dancing and what they were dancing to.

Wine was his destination and his only focus.

"Do you have any Edran wine?" He leaned heavily against the bar, wincing as he pulled a stool closer and sat on it.

The barkeep smiled. "This is Pastora, mate. Name your poison, and I'll give it to you by the bucketload."

"A cup will do fine. Bordaen red, please. The good stuff." In a second, there was a pewter cup in front of him, filled to the brim.

"Sir," said the barkeep, "can I ask you a question?" Sir Willam noticed he had a kind-looking face. The crow's feet by his eyes told him he had smiled a lot in his life. The salt-and-pepper hair told him he had stressed.

"Yes, she's a squin. They're real," said the knight, already knowing what he would ask.

"Of course they're real! But are their powers real? That's the question, innit?"

Sir Willam studied him deeper, thinking, *Can I trust him?*

Maybe he can help me with my mission. And everything told him yes, he can, and yes, he could. But then again, Sir Willam was not a great judge of character. Just yesterday, he had knowingly decided to trust a pirate and had climbed a mountain with him only to be attacked and then later taken hostage.

"No," he said, "their powers aren't real. A load of fairy tales. She is, however, a wonderful companion." At this, he stroked the top of her head with a finger. "Kind of a shit swimmer though." The squin pulled her head away and ran across his neck to his other shoulder.

"Shame," said the barkeep, "my mum used to tell me if I ever saw a squin, I should follow it and feed it a few coppers. I shoulda known that was bollocks. What brings you to Pastora?"

"I'm looking for a crew. I need strong people who are good workers and some mules. It's a . . . construction job . . . for Lord Barnum. My employer gave me a list of prospects." He figured he didn't need to trust the barkeep with fake information. Lies didn't come as naturally to him as they did to Yevnir, so he fumbled with his words.

"Mules are no trouble. There's a farmer in town who will lend them to you for free, if you tell him you're workin' for the lord. Workers won't be as easy, I fear. Let's have a look, then. I'd say I know all the locals in Biverna, some of the frequent travelers too."

The barkeep wiped his hands on an off-white apron while Sir Willam tried to shake off the rainwater from the little scroll Yevnir had given him. When he handed it over, the barkeep held it far from his face and peered down, trying to read the muddled letters.

"Ah, yes. These are good choices. Barasina and Figurt, the odd couple, as I call them. Both born with extra arms. Mad how they found each other, I think. I mean, in the whole world, two freaks run into each other on one tiny little island. What are the chances?"

"'Freaks' is a bit harsh, don't you think?" Sir Willam remembered the couple he'd seen sitting on the bench when he'd first walked through Biverna. They were undoubtedly different, but extra limbs seemed more like a blessing to Sir Willam than a deformity.

He wondered if they were human or some other race of creature he had never encountered before. They certainly looked human to him.

"I don't mean it as an insult. I quite like the pair. They're severely deformed though, no question about it. They live in the north part of town. Yellow door, big rose bushes on the roof. Y'can't miss it, really." The barkeep went on trying to read the list, although the ink was blotted and the names were clearly becoming harder to read as he went. "Oh, the whole clan, eh? The Brochmail Brothers. Savage little dwarves. Don't let them hear you say that word though, 'little.' You know how dwarves are about those things."

"I don't need your opinion on everybody, if you don't mind. Wondering if you know where I could find them," the knight said. Something about the way the bartender spoke made him uncomfortable. Was this how he talked about the beasts he had slain? He had a right to it though—they were monsters. Dwarves were not monsters.

"What? Did I offend you, Sir?" Suddenly the barkeep's face didn't seem so kind. The crow's feet were lost in a scrunched scowl.

"I've come for a drink and a little help. Call them what names you like. Although 'little dwarves' *is* redundant, is it not?"

"Oh, you Edrans are so touchy when it comes to words." The barkeep rolled his eyes and laughed until he realized Sir Willam wasn't laughing with him.

"Right, well, you'll see them around town ridin' dogs. By

their choice too! It isn't a trick or some cruel joke. They ride the beasts everywhere!"

The knight finished his cup, snatched the scroll from the barkeep's hands, then stood up to leave.

"Are you gonna pay for that?" the barkeep hollered when the knight was already halfway to the door.

"I'll send one of the Brochmail Brothers to settle my debt," he said without looking back.

Outside, he looked about the town, the mountain on his left and the sea to his right. Puddles polka-dotted the mud streets. Where there was cobble, it was darkened and waterlogged. The footprints from the children's ball game had been washed away. The clouds coming in from the west were a dark and bluish gray.

"I will not be caught in that muck again," the knight said aloud. "Let's get moving." The squin nuzzled into his collar and seemed to shrink at the sight of the incoming clouds.

"It'll be the odd couple first, I think. We don't have much of a choice." The streets were mostly bare, save for a few stragglers taking down their stands or covering their wares. There was something startling in its emptiness, how a town could go from bustling to barren in a moment's notice, from green to gray.

Stopping in the empty street, he admired the silence. He reveled in the fact he would be the one to face the storm, as he always had been, and at the same time he resented himself for it. From somewhere close and yet unknown to him, he heard a low growl. It shook him like the cold and sent his eyes darting around, investigating every alley, ditch, and roof.

On his shoulder, the squin growled back, trying to match the pitch of whatever had made the sound in the first place. Sir Willam turned his neck to try to see her, astounded by the vocal range of such a small creature. She was baring her teeth as she growled, snarled, and salivated.

It was both intimidating and adorable, and with her orange-and-black-striped fur she looked like the tiniest tiger any man had ever seen, although the knight had only ever seen one before.

"Now you decide to be brave?" said the knight. "Now?"

He reached across his body to stroke her head with one finger, still scanning the streets with his eyes.

"I thank you for your protection, little squin, but if something attacks us, let me be the brave one. You are far too precious to die a knight's death."

After that, he made quick work of finding the odd couple's cottage, eager for the shelter, both from the rain and from the source of that growl. The house was as the barkeep had described; the door was a bright and flaky yellow with a brass knob.

On either side of it were cobblestone walls sporting narrow windows like arrow slits, except paned with glass. The roof hung over slightly, so that even standing at the door his back was getting wet from the drops still sliding off it. There were rose bushes on the roof, but they were disheveled and some had been uprooted by the wind.

He stepped on a rose petal as he moved to knock on the door. His knocks were firm and loud. Somehow, he felt they might take him more seriously if he knocked with some exertion. It was the lady who answered the door.

"Hello," she said kindly. She had opened the door with one of her left arms, the other two busy combing her hair. The left arm that was in the normal position held her long brown hair, while the right arm was combing it. The third arm, which had opened the door, was on her left side, below the other one, at a level with her chest.

"Hi . . . hello. Are you Barasina?"

"Oh dear, it's another one. Honey!" She turned her neck

and slammed the door shut. Sir Willam looked around awkwardly, feeling like he'd caused a scene.

A moment later, the yellow door opened again. This time, Figurt was there too. "Have you no shame? No mercy?" spat Figurt.

"I'm not—"

"They sent you here to see the freaks, did they?" His eyes went wide, and he held up all four hands to wave them as he did a little hop and a skip. "Well, here we are! The seven-armed couple. The deformed. The grotesque!" As he said this, Barasina stood with two arms crossed and one down at her side. Her uncrossed arm played with the seam of her white dress.

"No, you misunderstand me. I—"

"What's that on your shoulder?" Barasina uncrossed her arms to point.

Sir Willam grabbed the squin and held it out gently. "She is a squin," he said. "I haven't come to gawk or to make fun. I've come to hire you for a job."

Figurt looked to Barasina and turned her away from the knight, using his other three hands to gesture for him to wait. They whispered something to each other and then turned back to him. "For a circus? Will we be the act before or after the squin?"

The knight let out a chortle and then said, "Would that make the difference? No, I'd like to hire you for something much less demeaning and far more rewarding." Their interest was clear enough on their faces, so he decided he could continue. "May I come in?"

...

By the hearth, he sipped gingerly from a scalding cup of tea, admiring the painting that hung over the mantel. It was of a ship, closer to the size of the *Sivkara* than the *Loyal Blue*, sailing through rough waters. The sails were a yellowish-white color and displayed no symbols or markings of fealty. The waves crashed in around it, water shooting over the taffrail and on to the portside deck. The sky looked much the same as the one outside their window, dark clouds looming above. But in the top-left corner, peeking through the black and spewing clouds, was the sun.

Their house smelled pleasantly of fresh-picked lavender, of which they had several bushels hanging by a window, and burning oak, which crackled in the hearth. He had taken off his boots and socks to dry, revealing toes so wrinkled they looked like a row of morel mushrooms. Barasina and Figurt sat across from him on their cushioned chairs, *her* knitting as if they had no company, and *him* staring with an accusatory eye at Sir Willam even as he lifted his cup to drink. Outside, the clouds had begun to purge their rain. Consistent pattering and sporadic booms of thunder played in the background of what Sir Willam felt to be the most unwelcome job interview that had ever taken place.

Figurt set his tea down on the end table between the two chairs. Folding his top two arms and resting the bottom two on the armrests, he leaned forward. His clean-shaven face flickered with the light of the fire. "Tell me, Sir Willam. Why did you consider us for this job?"

"I didn't. It was the Goldleaf. Do you know the name? Surely you would've run into him. Here." The knight pulled out the scroll from his robe and handed it to Figurt. "He put your name on this list."

Figurt took it in his top two hands. Almost immediately after unrolling the scroll, he showed it to Barasina. They shared a concerned look. Barasina shrugged. Figurt nodded. "We'll do it," they said together. Barasina put down her yarn and knitting needles and stoked the fire. Figurt picked up his tea and took a deep pull, sitting back into his chair.

"I have yet to tell you what the job is."

Figurt handed the scroll back to the knight. He unrolled it.

Will, these are the names you will need. It is imperative that you bring them all.

-Mr. and Mrs. Figurt Cortell

-Delvic Drunin (Be careful not to offend him)

-The Brochmail Brothers (Will come if Delvic is convinced)

-Miss Samantha Borteau

Good luck,

Yevnir

Figurt peered over the list as Sir Willam held it and tapped his finger on the last name. "Samantha Borteau," he said. "Nasty, evil witch. Lives on the edge of town in her little hovel. Last summer she tried to 'cure our illness' with a potion she snuck into our milk jug. As if it were an *illness!* I have tried to confront her about it several times now, but anytime I get close she disappears. If you can facilitate our meeting and make her listen to our piece, then we will do whatever job you need doing."

Sir Willam grimaced.

"And you think you can still work with this witch after you have confronted her? What if she doesn't have an answer for her actions? What if she is as evil as you say?"

Barasina's face twisted into a mean scowl. "Then we will kill her, and the job will go on."

Sir Willam nodded, slightly shocked. "Then I will be down a worker. Would you perhaps consider waiting until after the job to kill her, if she has no answer for you?" Seeing that Barasina was still considering the proposition, the knight looked to Figurt.

"Yes," Figurt confirmed, "if she has no excuse, then we will kill her once the job is done. Deal?"

Sitting back in his chair, the knight weighed his options, only to find he had none. Yevnir had been quite clear about needing every name on the list. If these were the conditions on which he would accomplish that, then he would have to accept it and move forward.

"Alright. I will find Miss Borteau and circle back to you. But I'd hate to see good people thrown in a cell or executed for killing a woman I put them in company with, and more so, I'd hate to be the cause of that woman's death."

Witches were a gray area for Sir Willam. On the rare occasions he had encountered hostile creatures—trolls, ghosts, serpents—he had had no trouble killing them. Monsters were monsters. Witches, though—well, they looked too human.

"Oh, the community won't mind," said Figurt. "The mayor is a crook. The Barnums and the Samhales on the other side of the island own him. Lord Barnum especially hates witches, anything with too many limbs, or limbs that are too short for his liking, and he's not alone in that hatred, is he, love?" The couple shared a look and a morbid chuckle. "The only people more hated than us in the community are Miss Borteau and those dwarves."

"Sounds like quite a plight. I'm sorry." The couple seemed to ignore this last sentiment, and Sir Willam felt his awkward plea for peace between them and the witch had gone completely over Figurt's head. He also made a mental note to ask the witch to curse Yev for giving him this list of hated Bivernians. "Thank you for the tea. I should be leaving now."

"Wait! You never introduced us to your squin. We have only ever heard of the creature. How did you come upon it?"

Sir Willam had already begun to put his socks back on. "She sort of found me. It's a long story. The Goldleaf is involved. You will understand better by the time the job is finished, but unfortunately, I am on a tight schedule." He continued with his socks, wiggling them, as they were still damp, over his wrinkled feet. Then he hurriedly put his boots on and stood. "I will be back. Hopefully soon."

The couple smiled excitedly. "Goodbye, Sir Willam," they said together.

CHAPTER NINE

He found Miss Borteau in a gravelly hut near the base of the mountain, east of the path he and Varro, the first mate of the Ahkovan pirate crew, had taken on his first day on the island. The hovel seemed to be leaning, and one side had half crumbled away, leaving a pile of rocks at the base of what used to be a much thicker wall. Her doorway was a tangle of vines hanging down from the roof to the wet grass beneath it. Upon closer inspection, these same vines seemed to run through the whole of the structure and may have been what kept it together, like some sort of living and expanding rope. Smoke spewed from a small mudbrick chimney, climbing in the moist air and disappearing in the calm and constant rain.

Sir Willam cleared his throat. "Miss Borteau," he said loudly, thinking it good practice to announce himself when approaching a witch. He heard a clank of pans and a pop, which threw a cloud of smoke from the chimney. His hand shot toward the hilt of his sword. Caution kept him from drawing.

"Who's there?" A woman's voice came from inside, as gravelly as her hut and filled with quakes of fear.

"My name is Sir Willam Hornsby. I have come to offer you a job."

He tried to bury the impatience in his voice. The rain, although much tamer than it had been earlier, was cold.

"Sir? I don't know any knights. I don't wanna know any knights."

"I have not come to offer you any ill will. Only work. May I please come inside?"

The pause lasted so long he had begun to think she had gone away, disappeared in the smoke that left her chimney.

In a hoarse and quiet voice, she said, "If you leave the blade where you stand."

Reluctantly, he unsheathed his sword and stuck it point down into the soft terrain. The vines that were the witch's doorway began to untwist and curl themselves up until the passage was clear. Inside was a darkness that reminded him of the hull on the pirate ship. Memories of his brief captivity made his entrance all the more terrifying.

He looked back before ducking into the hut. His sword stood there, sticking out of the mud like a monument to his old self. He sought his own reassurance one more time, whispering to himself, "You are the Sir Willam from the stories."

And the knight entered the witch's den.

It was not at all the hell he'd expected. The witch stood humpbacked over a table chopping something up and tossing pieces of it into a boiling pot. He could not see what she was chopping, but he imagined it was frog limbs, raven heads, or rat tails.

"Welcome, Sir," she said. Around her, an assortment of small animals hung by vines from the ceiling—squirrels, rabbits, a bat, the biggest being a badger.

She must put her game somewhere, thought the knight. *There's nothing wicked in that.*

"You are disappointed?" the witch presumed. He saw from the side of her face a smile that made his skin crawl. "You expected skulls and chalk spells on the walls. Perhaps a shriveled fetus in a jar?" she cackled, letting her head fall back a little then forward again to her work.

"Ma'am, I do not mean to offend you in any way, and if it is not true, I apologize for my believing in it, but I was told you are a witch."

She turned to him, revealing on the table a stock of cabbage she had been cutting. Sir Willam exhaled. Miss Borteau was a short and slender woman, slightly withering in her old age, with brittle-looking blond hair, wrinkled pale skin, and a tattered gray cloak tied at the waist with twine.

"Who told you this?" she spat.

Sir Willam took a step back, wondering if he could escape the range of her spells if she decided to use them. "A few people, ma'am. I apologize. Here, I was given a list with your name on it." He handed her Yevnir's scroll and watched as she read it.

The witch read with a frown. "I don't know what your list is for or what it had to do with you thinking I'm a witch, but I'm not interested."

"I'm sorry. But, if you are not a witch, would you happen to know why you are on this list?"

"I know some things others do not. That is true. For instance, I know that the squin hiding inside your collar has lived on this island longer than some of the trees it climbs on and that it wields magic that men are not fit to comprehend. I know that it trusts you, although I do not know why it allows you to use it. Those things I know. But 'witch' implies malice, and I haven't done a malicious thing. Not once in all my years, and there have been many."

The knight felt his shoulders drop and his arms loosen. "I

believe there can be good witches, though if you insist on avoiding the term, then it won't be tolerated on the job." Did he truly believe this, or was he saying it to appease her? He wasn't sure.

"Oh, how kind of you! Will you spare me, then, brave knight? Since I am one of the few good witches?" She rolled her eyes and handed back the list. "The job?"

"Yes. If you accept, I promise it will be worth your while."

Miss Borteau fell into a rocking chair by her fireplace. She reached down to a bowl at her feet and came up with a handful of a black and grainy powder. She leaned over and tossed it into the fire, and it sent sparks and smoke shooting through the chimney. Suddenly, Sir Willam felt warm again, completely dry.

"What is the job?" the witch asked.

"I'm afraid I can't tell you unless you accept it."

"And have you secured the employment of Barasina and Figurt?" She watched him intently, sitting forward slightly in her chair.

Reluctant to answer, Sir Willam swallowed. "They have agreed, yes. Actually, they said something about you. I believe they are under the impression that you poisoned their milk."

"I did not!" She stood, her nose scrunched. "Those fools! If their milk was poisoned, they would be dead. Did they not tell you the facts? This is how it happens, you see. I try to help, and it backfires. Then the rumors spread, and now I am here. An outcast to society. An Anchorite by all but affiliation."

He waited patiently with his arms folded, then said, "That is nothing short of an injustice! You must crave the chance to explain yourself."

The knight was quite confident by this point that Miss Borteau was, in fact, a witch. He had seen a similar scenario take place back in Edra, near Winderly. People mistrusted women with solutions, especially those without explanation.

Most of the time, in Sir Willam's experience, this mistrust was unwarranted. However, in rare cases, the people guessed right about a witch but did not wait to judge her intentions before deciding her fate.

This was the case with that poor old woman near Winderly, and the memory of his involvement in the situation gave him a feeling of guilt as he looked at Miss Borteau, like he was one of the people she was hiding away from in this secluded hut. He couldn't shield himself from the wave that fell over him. *She was a witch*, he thought. Even if she had good intentions, she was a danger to the people. He shouldn't have felt bad for what happened to her. Still, he couldn't shake this feeling. It was something like sadness, something like sympathy. He had to remind himself there was a lot at stake here.

Curious eyes stared back at him. A change in expression was all he needed. "I can give it to you," he said. "Your chance. I can make them listen. All you have to do is join my crew."

Miss Borteau came up with a quill from somewhere in her sleeve, or perhaps from thin air. She wrote her name in big letters next to the names of the multi-armed couple, never dipping her quill.

Smiling, Sir Willam took the paper from her and gave her a nod. "Meet us at dawn, at the foot of the mountain. Thank you." He turned to leave.

"You are a good friend to him."

Sir Willam stopped and turned his head.

"I am not sure he deserves it."

Sir Willam stared at her and felt uneasy. There was darkness behind her eyes and a slight smile tugging at the corners of her lips. She was standing now, her hands folded together at her waist. He nodded to her slowly, then ducked under the vines to leave the hut, thinking about what she had said. *How does she know about Yevnir?*

It was only sprinkling now, though the clouds were still

dark overhead. In front of him was a plain of mud, littered with puddles and patches of matted grass, and his sword was gone.

He stopped dead in his tracks only a few feet from the door.

His heart rate quickened. His eyes focused and darted back and forth from Bivernian dwellings to the tree line. He heard before he saw—a deep, cruel growl, like thunder if it lingered. Then the eyes—a dark yellow, almost like the orange of the squin's coat. The squin sank down into his cloak, using her claws to hang on to the space between his shoulder blades. He could hear his heart beating within him—*thump, thump*—so fast as if it wanted to run away. It met its crescendo at the sight of the first gray-haired paw stepping out from the darkness beneath the trees.

Sir Willam planted his feet, balled his fists, and gritted his teeth. "Show yourself!" he shouted.

Whatever came out from the shadows would have to be determined to kill him. He was not going to run away. He was prepared to fight tooth and nail for this inconsequential spot, his feet planted in the mud as if Yevnir's treasure was buried beneath it, for no other reason than because it was what he expected of himself.

The bushes and low-hanging trees shook, answering his request. Huge, ferocious-looking gray dogs with dwarves upon their backs appeared from within the forest. The biggest, meanest-looking one trotted to the middle of the yard, drooling and smiling, if dogs smiled. It had scars along one side, puncture wounds and slashes, and its eyes were as wild as the squin's. It bared its teeth and uttered its deep growl once more.

The dwarf riding it was a contradiction. He looked refined, put together, wearing a light-green embroidered tunic with a gold pin. All the hair on his head was shaven besides a block of black on his chin, and dangling from his hip was a short sword with a bronze hilt.

He tugged on its gray fur and the dog straightened from its

hunched, stalking stance and meandered toward Sir Willam at a leisurely pace, its owner holding his head high and raising the knight's sword in one hand.

"Is it this yer lookin' for?" The dwarf tossed the sword in the mud, halfway between Sir Willam and himself.

Sir Willam straightened. A big smile came across his face and he started to laugh. "I'm sorry. I apologize." He was bent over now, his hands on his knees. Even putting his hand to his mouth couldn't stop his laughter.

The dwarf in front of him looked around at his comrades. His cocky grin quickly turned into a frown, which morphed into a scowl. "You laugh? Never seen a dwarf before? He laughs at us!"

"No, no, not at you!" Sir Willam put a hand up but continued his laughter.

"I'm no dancin' dwarf, knight. That's the first thing you'll come to know about me."

Finally, Sir Willam was able to straighten his posture again, wiping the tears from his eyes with a knuckle and letting the last chuckles leave him.

"I know you aren't a dancing dwarf, Mister Drunin. I've just remembered myself, is all. You see, I haven't been myself lately." He strode over to his sword and picked it up from the mud. Wiping it on his cloak, he grinned at the dwarf. "Thank you for reminding me."

"So, you know who I am, then?"

"Oh, yes, Delvic, I know who you are. And I see that the Brothers are many. May I ask why you ambush me so?"

The dwarf looked past him to Miss Borteau's hut. "Yer conspirin' with witches, are ya?"

"Not conspiring, no. Is that why you followed me here? Took my sword? Because of the witch?"

"And because of those freaks with the arms." When he said this, the other dwarves nodded in agreement atop their dogs.

Sir Willam watched their faces then looked to the sky and laughed, shaking his head. “Yev, you clever bastard.”

Looking back at the leader of the Brochmail Brothers, he said, “My name is Sir Willam Hornsby. I have a job for all of you.”

CHAPTER TEN

Dawn of the Next Day

Sir Willam rubbed the sleep from his eyes. He sat leaning against the neck of a workhorse, gripping three ropes in one hand that each led to the reins of a different donkey. "They will be here," he told the horse. "Don't worry."

The squin stood tall on the back of the horse. If she was trying to be a lookout, she was looking the wrong way, staring at the looming Hollow Mountain and glancing occasionally at the dense forest on either side of its base. When he turned in his saddle to see her, she was peering up at the mountain's peak, although from this close she couldn't see it.

"Are you thinking of home?" he asked, receiving no response. He nodded to himself. "You are thinking of family. I know . . . We are told we must help our friends and be loyal to them, and we are told the same of our blood. We cannot be in two places at once, cannot always help one without neglecting the other. We are only human! Well, you are not human, but the same applies. Eh, you can't understand a word I say." He sighed. "But you feel it too. I know you do."

The couple was the first to arrive, satchels on their backs, walking sticks in hand, and cheerful expressions on their faces. The Brochmail Brothers followed close behind, skulking out of the shadows on their dogs and closing in on him as they had at the witch's hut. Now it was only the witch they were waiting on.

Barasina and Figurt mounted the donkeys happily, leaving their walking sticks in the dirt. Sir Willam tied the reins of the third donkey to a tree. The Brochmail Brothers waited impatiently atop their own mounts, shooting disdainful and perhaps disgusted looks at the couple. Their leader, with his bald head and black chin beard, glanced at Sir Willam from time to time as they waited, as if to say, "You see? I knew she wouldn't come."

"She will be here," Sir Willam announced. "Let's all be patient."

"You cannot trust a witch, Sir. She would sooner see us all die than work with us. I knew this was a bad idea," said Barasina.

Delvic perked up and chuckled. "I'd have to say I agree with the freak."

"Freak?" Figurt drew a knife in two of his four hands. "No man will call my wife a freak, especially not a dwarf."

That sparked a roar of grumbling and disapproving remarks through the gathering of Brochmail Brothers. The leader happily drew his short sword.

Sir Willam could do nothing but shake his head. If this came to blows, he knew he would be helpless to stop it. There were too many of the dwarves, and too many hands to stay where the couple was concerned.

"Yes, yes, we are all freaks." A booming voice came from the direction of the mountain, so loud it seemed the mountain itself was talking. When he turned, he saw Miss Borteau on a huge black steed. She looked twice the size she had been in her cabin. Her back stood tall where it had hunched before; a tall, pointed hat crowned her head; and a flowing purple cloak drooped to her horse's midsection. "Haven't you all heard it enough in your lives?" Her voice was softer now, motherly. "I know *I* have. I've heard it all my years, and there have been many. Is it too much to ask, that in the company of fellow freaks, we can be as equals?"

Silence followed. Sir Willam glanced around, wondering, hoping for someone to say something.

Finally, Barasina spoke up. "Let's have it, then, your explanation. We can't be equals until you tell us what you were doing meddling with our milk."

"That was not what it seemed."

"You tried to poison us!" Figurt shouted. "I'll rip your head from your body when I get the chance. I swear it on the gods, and not a man, dwarf, or giant will stop me."

Barasina nudged her donkey closer to the witch and pointed a finger at her. "And I'll start the fire while he does it. Your ashes will rise to Silas and you'll never feast in Oros's halls. You'll never get to—"

"It was a remedy, my dear . . ." the witch said with a soft frown, ". . . for the child."

Barasina revolted, her eyes filling with tears. "What? What child?" Figurt reached out and steadied her donkey, catching her gaze.

"The people were talking," Miss Borteau explained. "Everyone in Biverna knew you were trying. That so-called healer spread it as soon as you went to her for help. They all talked. They thought it was abominable. They thought it was unnatural, that people like you and your husband should get to have a child."

Barasina was crying now, the tears running down her cheek faster than she could wipe them even with her three hands. Figurt did his best to comfort her. Everybody else stayed where they were. Sir Willam was shocked by the quietness of the dogs, and he felt a sort of embarrassment for forcing this to happen in front of all of the Brochmail Brothers. This was a moment not meant for him or the dwarves, but there was no stopping it once it had started.

"What could be more natural than wanting a child?" said the witch. "What could be purer? I wanted to help you, but I knew you would turn me away if I offered, probably shout at me to make sure the neighbors knew where you stood—that you weren't my friend. They all do it. It's alright, dear. I have been chased and mobbed, beaten and spit on. When you saw me in the kitchen . . . I was scared. I couldn't explain myself, could I? You wouldn't have listened."

Through a sob, Barasina asked, "Would it still work?"

Miss Borteau responded with a nod.

"Sir Willam showed me the list," said the witch. "I thought, maybe if he gave us the opportunity to explain ourselves away from prying eyes, this job would be worth doing. I came so I could do a little bit of good, even if it is only our company who knows about it." From her sleeve slid a little clear vial with a green pulpy substance inside and a small wooden stopper at the top. "Drink this. Half before and half after." She looked between Barasina and her husband. "And a child will come."

To Sir Willam's surprise, Barasina climbed down from her donkey and Miss Borteau did the same. Meeting in the middle, they gave each other a hug. A cloaky, army hug, and the witch's hat fell from her head. She gave Barasina the vial as they broke from their hug, and she took it in all three hands, holding it up in front of her face with tears streaming from her eyes.

"Thank you," she cried. Figurt came to her side and took his wife up in his four arms in a fully enveloping embrace, nodding gratefully to Miss Borteau.

Delvic Drunin was the first to clap, then his brothers started in. "Well done," Delvic exclaimed, wiping a tear from his eye. "Bloody well done!"

Sir Willam smiled. *I may do some good here after all*, he

thought. *It'll have to make up for saving Yev 'cause that will surely count against me.* Then, to everybody, and with his most authoritative voice, he said, "Now that we're all friends and freaks together, I think it is time I told you what the job is."

Figurt and Barasina parted from their hug, tears still dampening their cheeks. Delvic sniffed and wiped his eyes again as he straightened his posture, giving a quick grin back to his brothers, who seemed to have multiplied since Sir Willam last gauged their number.

"Go on, then, knight," Delvic encouraged. "You've promised me riches. Now tell us what to do and see how a dwarf can outwork any other."

Turning in his saddle, Sir Willam gently scooped up the squin into the palm of his hand, keeping her by his hip. "You all will know what this creature is. If you don't remember, think about the stories your mothers told you in the late hours of the night. Fantasies. Fairytales . . ." Holding the squin out in front of him, he said, "Reality."

The knight took great pleasure in the shocked expressions on the dwarves' faces. He continued with a smirk, "Your mothers may have told you of a squin's power, but if not, this one will soon remind you."

He tilted his palm and let her scurry down the horse's leg and into the grass. She looked up at him with wide eyes, and he reached into the pocket of his cloak, digging out the coin. He tossed it down to her as the dwarves, the witch, and the multi-armed couple all watched intently. The squin took it into her mouth, gnawed on it, twisted it in her hands, then darted off into the woods on the south side of the mountain.

"You know what to do!" he shouted.

The dogs bolted after her, twenty bright-eyed dwarves bouncing in their saddles. Sir Willam put a hand down to help the witch onto her steed. She looked up at him with the same mischievous look she'd had in her hut. "Gold doesn't come without blood, Sir Willam. Tell me, when you leave this island, what consequences will you let stay here? Who will face them?"

He frowned, squinting slightly. "There will be no consequences. Everybody will get their share, and they will all go their separate ways."

"Is that so?" she snickered. "Do you know what the Brochmail Brothers do? Did the Goldleaf not tell you? Or did you not care to ask?"

He sucked his teeth and said, "We have to go." She eyed him before they took off together. Her face seemed younger now, more alive, as if fresh air was all it took to tighten her loose skin. They followed the dwarves into the woods, Barasina and Figurt on their tails, and the third donkey they left there in the clearing.

Through the woods they trekked, squeezing between low-hanging branches and stomping through the damp undergrowth. The dwarves were out of sight, but their trail was impossible to lose. In their dogs' lustful chasing, they had kicked up a path like a ravine. Sir Willam ducked under a spindly branch that still caught his cloak, and the workhorse below him would have left him hanging behind if he hadn't managed to rip himself free in time.

"There are some advantages in being a dwarf, I think." With his free hand, he felt the hood of his cloak to find the hole the branch had opened. He shook his head and carried on, telling himself there would be gold enough to mend it at the end of this trail.

Through the trees, they could still see the base of the mountain on their right. On this side it was rocky but still with patches of green. Moss hung from its ledges and grass carpeted its occasional slope. The knight barely dodged another low branch as he admired the mountain from a distance. There were mountains in Edra, of course—the Barolins, the Edrans, the Sentanis—but none of them quite matched this one's stubbornness for life. It clung on to the color green as if it itself were a colossal pyramid-shaped plant.

When he turned his head to check on Miss Borteau, he found her staring at him. He swallowed. Her brown eyes seemed to peer through him, as if she were watching the inner workings of his brain. She smiled.

Something moved behind her.

He reached for his sword as his neck craned and he squinted to see it. Twenty paces away, a row of antlers jutted out from a tree, followed by an almond-colored body bigger than the witch's steed. Cobwebs connected its many points and moss hung down by its ears. It was the elk from the mountain, the one he had stopped Varro from killing. As quickly as it came into view, it disappeared again, bounding away until the forest swallowed it whole.

The witch never turned to look, never stopped staring at him with that knowing smile.

"Miss Borteau?" Sir Willam said.

"Yes?"

"How did you know about Yevnir? About our friendship?"

"What do you mean?"

"You said I was a good friend to him, and you weren't sure he deserved it."

The witch raised an eyebrow and shook her head at him. "I wasn't talking to you."

Sir Willam looked away from her with squinted eyes, back toward the path ahead of them. The mountain was coming into view again through the tops of the trees. *If she wasn't talking to me, then she was talking to the squin.* When he glanced to his side, Miss Borteau was still watching him.

"We have to speed up," he said, trying to get her to stop staring. "I don't want those dogs eating the squin if they catch her too fast. Come on." He slapped his reins and barreled through the branches in front of him, letting the leaves and twigs tear at him rather than suffering the witch's gaze.

As they went on, the trail seemed to pull them closer to the mountain's base. Barasina and Figurt were slower than the rest of the group on their donkeys, but Sir Willam made sure they were never out of sight so that when they finally caught up with the dwarves and their dogs, the multiarmed couple was not too far behind.

They huddled together facing the mountain, the dogs panting vigorously and drooling from open mouths and dangling tongues. Sir Willam watched Delvic separate himself from the pack and ride toward him and Miss Borteau.

"Look, knight!" he called, gesturing to the mountain. "Our little creature has found it!"

Over the dwarves' heads, he could see the top of a round indent in the rock face. Vines clung to the rock around it and hung freely from the overhang, breaking up the darkness beyond with green lines and spots of red where little flowers sprouted. He nudged his horse forward.

This is it, then, Yev? he thought. *This is where your friend hid it?*

As he approached the mouth of the cave, the Brochmail Brothers parted for him, yanking at their dogs' leads to wake them from their ravenous delirium. All that could be seen through the vines was an empty blackness. He approached it cautiously, thinking there had to be some sort of catch. *Yev wouldn't just throw all his treasure in a cave with nothing to protect it. Then again, it wasn't Yev who hid it.* From beneath the vines came a little orange creature. The squin escaped the darkness slowly, her back looking crimson as the shadow clung to her body and then to her tail.

With a smile, the knight climbed down from his saddle. They met halfway, sandwiched by a company of self-declared freaks and a cave full of treasure. Sir Willam knelt in front of her, holding out a hand for her to climb into. Instead, she dropped something cold and heavy from her mouth into his hand. He looked down at it. A ring. A thick band of gold with a dazzling rectangular diamond.

He closed his fist and stood, facing the company. "Barasina, Figurt, in your saddle bags, there are a bundle of sacks." He grabbed the unlit torch protruding from his own saddle bag and rummaged for his flint. "Get them and hand them out. I will be back." Striking his flint, he pushed through the curtain of flowering vines into the darkness beyond.

The squin scurried between his legs, stopping in front of him to look back. "Go on, girl."

He followed her with his eyes until her little legs trampled a pile of gold. The sound the gold made when her back foot pushed off the coin beneath it, a *clang* and a *ting*, and the reflection of the sun through the vines barely shining on the coins would have made Yevnir shiver with excitement.

It would have made Willam's own brothers throw their fishing poles in the pond and dive to the floor, not knowing that what they had was the real treasure. Not knowing that he would leave it here in the cave if he could. That he would rather be fishing than looking for gold. That the fish were not the treasure but the fishing itself, and that it all meant nothing because he was here in Pastora rather than at home in Horntree with them.

He followed the little squin nonetheless. With his arm rising, fire stretched across a cavern with no end. The torchlight bounced and reflected through the space like an echo, giving back to the shadow with every flicker only to consume again. An unorganized heap of treasures sprawled out before him. Mounds of gold coins, bejeweled chalices, rubies, diamonds, and sapphires stretched back farther than his light could reach. How did all of this get here? He never could have imagined it would be this much.

Trudging through currency, his foot found something immovable, and he dug through the gold to find it. Brushing aside the minted faces of unfamiliar kings, noble and regal in their side profiles or eternally sitting on their thrones, he came upon something dark and jagged. He pulled it from their royal grasp, and it immediately turned green in the firelight. It was both reflective and translucent, gleaming, and clinging desperately to the blackness beneath it.

It was a statue of a faceless person.

This thing alone could buy the village in which he was raised, could hire enough men to burn it to the ground and rebuild it in gold. Why was this his first thought? None in his company or on the entirety of the island knew where his village was across the Callaseen Strait, and if they did they would have no reason to burn it, no reason to take it from him. Still, he stared down at this man of pure emerald and hated him for his worth. He unpinned his cloak, wrapped the statue in it, then pushed on through the cave.

The squin was out of sight, but he could hear her scampering through the field of treasures. When he raised his torch above his head, he finally saw the cave's end. Dripping stalactites reached down from the ceiling to their stalagmite lovers. As he came closer, he felt their drops—cold on his brow, the taste of minerals on his tongue. The squin sat there at the end, perched upon some large chest fenced off by stalagmites and threatening to be crushed or warped by the stalactite spikes that hung over it. Barnacle-looking moss covered this chest, as if it came up from the sea, covered in green algae like the rest of the island.

"What is it?" he asked the squin. "What have you found?"

Sir Willam stepped over and between a pair of stalagmites to get to her. The chest was long, made of some dark, rotting wood, and bordered with rusted iron. She jumped from the chest to his chest and climbed onto his shoulder. He carefully tried the latch. There was an ancient lock, rusted into a blob of orange-red iron. He blew crumbling rust out of an indentation he had felt with his thumb, then, finding the indentation to be a small letter "A," he scraped curiously to reveal the rest of the word.

Taking out his dagger, he tried to gently trace and carve out the next letter, and unlooping his waterskin from his belt, he gently poured a stream over the whole of the word until it read, "Attun." He stepped back. *It couldn't be*, he thought—the same word he had grown up saying with the priests back in Horntree. Half of a phrase that was his village's motto, their only prayer. It was a coincidence, he concluded. There can only be so many combinations of letters. There must be many words of the same spelling in different languages. It couldn't be the same word.

With this decided, he tried the lock again. Even with his gentle pull, the rotten wood around the lock gave way and the top came ajar slightly. With both hands free now, setting the Emerald Man on the damp stone and nestling his torch into a divot in the cave wall, he pushed the lid up until it cracked and broke off.

Inside was a bundled pile of dirty white linen. He reached in, almost laughing at the idea that he had come upon some ancient lady's clothing trunk, until he felt something solid. With a curious leer, he pushed aside the linens. He grasped something sharp and pulled it back swiftly. Blood seeped down from his palm to his wrist then dripped, like the mountain water from the stalactite, onto the cave floor.

Reaching back in, more carefully this time, he uncovered what had cut him—a black blade with a bare wood handle. He picked it up carefully, expecting the wood to rot away in his hand and the metal to crumble to dust in midair. It did not. He held it up to the torchlight. The pommel was a small silver tree, a familiar tree, with two types of branches, one regular and one spiked.

Willam recognized it immediately. The trees from his home village existed nowhere else. He felt the brooch that held his cloak together then pressed his finger into the little silver spike on the sword pommel until it drew a drop of blood.

"It is all a coincidence," he said to himself. "The spikes might not represent the horn trees from home. Maybe they are just a practical detail."

Then he inspected the blade, dark gray and not black as he had originally thought. He held it up closer to the light, felt the weight of it, the balance and its edge, until he saw something peculiar—an engraving along the side of the blade.

He blew a bit of dust from the indents, wiped it with his sleeve, then read it, clear as day: "Nagri Attun." And the phrase was completed.

CHAPTER ELEVEN

"Took you long enough, knight," Delvic said. "What are we waiting for?"

Sir Willam stood in front of the entrance to the cave, sword in one hand and torch in the other. The Emerald Man hung heavy, stuffed into a coin pouch not nearly big enough for it at the back of his belt. The squin had hopped down from his shoulder and was still clanging around in her city of gold, biting but never chewing on the various coins and trinkets.

Everyone had climbed down from their mounts and was ready to fill their bags, but even with twenty dwarves, a multi-armed couple, and a witch, they wouldn't have enough manpower to take all this treasure with them.

"Fill your bags with jewels before coins. They are worth more."

Every face in the company lit up at this confirmation of what they already knew was waiting in that cave. They rushed past him like children after sweets, their empty sacks ready to be filled. Miss Borteau was the last. She sauntered forward and stopped in front of him.

"I will carry this out for you," she said, "because you gave me an opportunity to be heard, and I gave you my word. But I must say now what I won't have the chance to later. This is a mistake, Sir Willam. No matter how you choose to split it between us, no matter how much you decide to take for yourself or for your conniving friend, it will all go to those dwarves in the end. Delvic is ruthless, and although many of his brothers are less so, it won't matter if he is allowed to live."

She tried to follow the rest under the vines, but Sir Willam dropped his sword and grabbed her arm.

"Unhand me. Now." Her eyes were burning, her veins pulsing with whatever spell she was ready to put upon him. He imagined she was about to incinerate him or turn him into cattle. He didn't care.

"What are you saying? Because it is different now than it was before."

She leaned into him, looked past the vines into the cave as the dwarves lit their torches, and whispered, "You must kill Delvic, or he will kill you, me, and that poor couple in there. Tell me, how will you save the Goldleaf if you are dead? How will you go fishing with your brothers?"

He shoved her away, scowling and clenching his jaw. "How do you . . . It doesn't matter! I won't kill a man in my employment."

"Then you will kill the rest of us. You will kill your friend. I can help you—"

"Nobody is going to die!"

The witch laughed maniacally. "You and your friend thought you could come to this island and take and disrupt and that somehow you would fly through us as fast as a falcon without losing a feather, but mark my words. Greed, gold, and loyalty . . . these are all things that come with a price. Someone will die because of your friend. You will not come out of this clean, knight, but you may still make it out alive if you listen. Kill the dwarf, and we will all live. Do what must be done."

“Are you two going to join us?” Barasina’s voice came from behind the vines. She parted them with all three of her hands and poked her head through.

“Yes, dear,” said the witch, “we’re right behind you.” She smiled at Barasina and stepped forward to follow her in. Right before she entered the cave, she looked back at Sir Willam and gave him a solemn nod.

He bent down and picked up the sword, shaking his head. “I will not kill Delvic for a witch’s superstition,” he said to himself. “I could not live with it. She can’t know for sure he will take everything for himself.” But beneath these affirmations of honor and integrity was a seed of doubt. How did she know about his brothers? How did she know about his and Yevnir’s relationship back in her hut? Surely, she was joking about talking to the squin. And if she knew all of that, did she know this too?

Unsheathing his old sword, Sir Willam tested the fit of this ancient sword in the black leather of his scabbard. A little loose. This dark blade was less bulky than the steel he was used to. Thinner. Sharper. He placed his hand on the hilt, his fingers closing around the rough wood. He tested its draw, expecting splinters in his palm but holding the blade out in front of him with pleasant, splinterless surprise. Next was the balance. He held it in one hand below the cross guard and moved it from side to side like a pendulum. The sword stayed horizontal, not tipping to one side or the other. Perfect.

If he weren’t still thinking of the witch’s words, he might’ve smiled. It was not every day a knight found a sword so fitting to him. His old one was perfectly adequate. There was no telling how many times it had served him faithfully. But the sword he now held was of a different caliber.

“Attun,” he said, holding the dark blade up into the light. “That is the word carved onto your chest. Is that your name, noble blade? I will have to ask the priests how you might’ve gotten such a name when I go home. If I make it home . . ." He sheathed Attun, and taking the Emerald Man from his coin pouch, he buried it at the bottom of his saddle bag. Then he wrapped his old sword in his cloak and tied it to his saddle, patting his horse's side as he finished.

He was facing the woods now, rather than the cave, and it was in the woods he saw it again. The elk. Peering from between a V-shaped tree, it made eye contact and then bounded away again. Sir Willam had the urge to follow but scoffed the urge away, shaking his head. He had fallen for that trick before. He would be following no more odd creatures through the Pastoran wood. Not in this lifetime.

So, turning, he delved back into the depths. Sword in scabbard, torch in one hand, and empty sack in the other. He pushed the vines from his path, careful not to lick them with his torch, and saw his company at work. The Brochmail Brothers were scattered, playing with the treasure trove as if it were a sandbox. Barasina and Figurt did the same, laughing joyously with the dwarves as they threw the coins in the air and pretended to drink from golden chalices or eat from silver plates. Delvic had a crown on his head with a row of at least thirty triangular diamonds in the band, and a necklace with as many sapphires. Sir Willam couldn't help but smile at this, but his smile quickly faded when Delvic spoke.

"I am the king! You hear me? Bow to King Delvic of the Brochmail clan!"

He raised his arm in regal display, a smug grin plastered on his face as he closed his eyes and breathed in his own imagined greatness.

"Let's get to work," declared the knight. And so they did, each of them sifting through the piles of gold to sort out the jewels. A moment of such privileged pickiness was almost comical. The eldest looking of the Brochmail Brothers—that is, those with the grayest beards—snickered at the youngsters as they filled their pockets with every sort of treasure before they even touched their bags. Seeing this brought up a question the knight had never thought to ask. He came up to a dwarf who sifted treasure alone, hiding away in a back corner of the cave, and pretended he came over to sift for jewels.

"Can I ask you something?" He looked at the dwarf on a knee, so that when the dwarf stood tall, they were at eye level with each other. The dwarf was bald with a veiny head and a long, shining black beard that reached almost to his belt.

"You're the boss, are you not?" the dwarf replied.

"Are you all actually brothers? Or is that more of a title?"

"We share the blood of the old dwarves, those whom your kind pushed into the forest and the mountain—and the ocean when they weren't so lucky. Not of the same mother, no. But children of the same origin nonetheless."

Sir Willam was taken aback by the way this dwarf spoke. He seemed more like a scholar than a criminal, like he would sooner read a book than rob a man. "My kind? Do you mean men? Or Edrans?"

The dwarf looked at the horn tree brooch pinning Sir Willam's cloak together, then he looked at his new sword and nodded to it. "You know of whom I speak."

He looked at the hilt of his sword, remembered the words engraved on it, and thought, *Either he knows something I do not, or he doesn't know what he is talking about at all.*

Then he said, "I am truly sorry for whatever my kind has done to you, good fellow. I hope these jewels and this gold can serve as some sort of penance, if even of the meager sort. May I ask, why is Delvic your leader? He is not the oldest, and I see now he is not the smartest. So why him?"

"A man from Edra could never understand such things. Dwarves there are few. Groveling, begging at the feet of taller men, lesser men. Here we do not grovel. Here we do not beg. That is because of Delvic Drunin."

"That is another thing . . . Drunin. You are called the Brochmail Brothers. Do any of you actually carry the name?"

"Our name is an homage to the original Brochmail." The dwarf bent slightly and picked up a Gramon gold, wiped it clean with a finger, and slid it into his pocket. "He was one of the few dwarves on the island who stayed when staying was perilous. He fought your ancestors tooth and nail."

"He was a hero, then? A legend? We have a few of our own where I am from."

"Your heroes put the village to torch. Brochmail brought the water bucket," the dwarf said, somewhat disdainfully.

"No. You have the wrong idea of my ancestors, friend."

The dwarf chuckled. "You have no connection to your ancestors, do you?"

"Do any of us?"

The dwarf pointed toward Delvic. "My connection is right there. Still fighting the same fight as Brochmail the Defiant."

Sir Willam turned his head looking for the dwarven leader but saw Miss Borteau instead. She stood on a pile of coins, her feet firmly planted on the flat lid of an old chest. She was looking up at the ceiling, tossing coins at it. To his amazement, these coins didn't bounce off the rock and come down again but instead stuck there. He stopped now to watch, as did the others. When she had thrown a fortune's worth of gold and a handful of jewels, she threw up her torch. It disappeared on the dripping black ceiling of the cave, and the coins and jewels shot out the light of its fire in beams so that the whole cave was lit up with a dull orange glow. The witch climbed down from her pile, delighted with herself.

That was when he saw Delvic.

"Delvic, no!"

The dwarf lunged, slashing wildly and screaming, "Witch! Die, witch!"

She stumbled and fell backward onto the pile of gold. His

sword came within inches of her face before Figurt smacked it away with a golden plate. Delvic swung at Figurt now, who stepped away, hitting the dwarf with a barrage of coins from three of his four hands.

The other Brochmail Brothers rushed to aid their leader, but Miss Borteau flung her arms out to the side and sent a wave of treasures flying in every direction to hinder their approach. Sir Willam dodged a chalice and took a few coins to the face and chest. He pushed on and made it to Delvic before the other dwarves.

"Stop this!" he yelled. "No one is going to die today!"

Delvic took a swing at him and he dodged it as his own sword flung from its scabbard. He held it in both hands, defensively.

"How much of this gold do you think my ancestors mined?" spat the dwarf. "You think I'm gonna let you lot run off with it?"

Miss Borteau made a gesture like she was about to send a fireball at the dwarf, but Sir Willam let go of his sword with one hand and raised it to tell her to stop.

"Delvic, I'm sorry. Alright? I'm sorry. I know you have hurt, that all dwarves have, and that this gold belongs to you before any man, but Lord Barnum is expecting it. You are working for *him*, not me. Now, I've told him I will need to pay my company handsomely for their efforts, so you will all leave here rich men and women, but take any more than I give you, and you are stealing from him. Are you prepared to take on a lord? Because I have seen what his men are capable of, and I don't think you are."

The dwarves had stopped their approach completely now. Delvic stayed his hand, and the knight continued, "You have nineteen men at your side. Brothers. Lord Barnum will kill them all if you betray your contract. Look, Delvic, I am trying to help my friend. I don't want this. You can take my share as well. No killing. Please."

Delvic's short sword clinked as he sheathed it. "You should've told us Lord Barnum was involved. But I can see why ya kept that bit to yerself. None of us woulda come." Then, looking away from the knight, he said, "Come on, lads. Time fer us to leave."

The dwarves obeyed immediately, hauling their bags of jewels over their shoulders but only walking a few steps toward the cave's entrance before Sir Willam interjected.

"I'm sorry, Delvic, all of you, but you cannot leave."

"And why the hell not?" A burly, gray-bearded dwarf snickered.

"I've told you. Lord Barnum will know. He has seen the list. If you do not show up at Arduny, he will track you down."

One by one, the dwarves walked past him, some chuckling, some waving away his comment with a hand, and others patting him on the arm as they ascended the gradual slope of treasures by his side. He grabbed the shoulder of the well-spoken dwarf he had talked to moments ago. "Do none of you care for your lives? Lord Barnum will kill you!"

The black-bearded dwarf looked up at him with something like pity. "You haven't done your research, friend. Or perhaps you have not been listening. We are outlaws—criminals, some would say. We cannot go to Arduny Castle. We would never leave there alive. Lord Barnum already hunts us . . . Your kind always has."

He grabbed Sir Willam's shoulder and squeezed it, giving him a nod before he walked past. There was a sadness in the gesture, a resignation of power over the world. The knight felt ashamed of himself, although he wasn't sure he had done anything to deserve this shame.

He could do nothing but watch as the Brochmail Brothers made their way through the vines and out into the open air, taking half of the cave's value with them. It was true he had not done his research. This whole week in Pastora he had been blindly moving from one disaster to the next. Now he had four people to do the work of a few dozen.

Even if they could fill all of the bags, two donkeys and two horses would not be able to carry the immense weight of it all. There would have been gold left behind even with the help of the dwarves, but approached with the fortune in jewels they would've brought to Arduny Castle, Lord Barnum would have been sure to release Yevnir.

The four of them who remained stood in a circle doing nothing until Figurt spoke, "We would still love our cut, Sir. But we're not exactly sure how we can bring all of this to Arduny. It's quite the journey as it is."

"I know. We will have to find another way, employ more people."

"I know people who would be willing," said Barasina. "By Oros, I'd think everybody in Biverna would be willing."

"Willing, but will they keep it to themselves? If too many know of this, they will take it. Someone will come along, and they won't be scared away by the threat of Lord Barnum, and they won't be so kind as to leave us living like the dwarves have," Miss Borteau warned. "They will take it and sail away. Someone like, say . . . a pirate."

She looked knowingly into Sir Willam's eyes.

He ran his hand through his hair, squeezing, wanting to pull it from his scalp as if it were the cause of his frustration. Then he took a deep breath and closed his eyes for a second. Her comment felt like an insult. She was in his head somehow, or else she had been following him. It didn't matter right now; he had to shift his focus to the current predicament.

It felt like there were no more options. He could leave, in theory, hire another merchant ship, and sail home. Yevnir had gotten himself into this mess, and it was not his responsibility to save him. He knew he could never bring himself to do it though, so the thought only brought on more frustration. He searched for anything else. His thoughts began to spiral. Why could nothing go according to plan? Anger built inside him—toward Yevnir, toward Delvic and the witch, and toward this damnable island—until he blurted, "You have the answer!"

He opened his eyes to see her, digging his heels into the gold coins beneath them and finding comfort in standing his ground. The witch glared back at him, her appearance ever changing since that ragged hut. Now she all but sparkled with youth. Her pale skin had regained a lively color, and her brittle blond hair had softened and smoothed so that it flowed like water instead of jutting down like the stalactites overhead.

"I have no answers for you, Sir." She grimaced. "Do not put the blame on yourself. There are some men not even the gods can save from their fates. What chance did you have?"

"The gods?" In his mind, he grabbed her throat and squeezed until she choked on her own words, spitting and clawing and kicking for her life. "Don't speak of your gods to me. Show me an altar for Oros or Eben, and I will piss on the stone," he laughed. "Show me a temple of Silas and I will fill it with whores!"

Barasina and Figurt stepped away from him, scowling. The witch only smiled.

"Your gods are as real as your foresight," said the knight. "You said Delvic would kill us if we didn't kill him first. *You* said that! And did he? No. No one died. You were wrong, and you know nothing that you say you do. Pirates? Pastora is full of pirates. They love it here. So much treasure and no one with the will to defend it. That's how you knew I'd run into pirates. Every other person on this green chamber pot is a damned pirate. You are no oracle, no great sorceress, merely a hag with a few tricks."

She glared at him.

"A freak? Go on, Sir Willam, you can say it. You have called me a hag, denounced and defiled the divine. Please, stoop lower. Call me a freak. Show us what knighthood means in Edra. Honor and chivalry, do they mean anything to you? Have they ever? You came into your knighthood through lies, didn't you? Were your vows just a few more, then? Show us who you really are!"

Sir Willam gripped his sword tight and pulled . . .

Through the vines came a chorus of shouts and desperate squeals. The four looked up toward the cave entrance.

"We will settle this, witch," said the knight, and together they followed the noise.

CHAPTER TWELVE

Sir Willam burst through the vines with his sword drawn. In front of him, the Brochmail Brothers were positioned in a semicircle, all of them on their back feet, weapons raised and their dogs growling a low tune beside them. Over their heads and between their ranks was a sight Sir Willam had already learned to dread. Green robes and capes partially covered the steel armor of Lord Barnum's men. Long spears and pikes filled the space between the dwarves and their human enemies, all of them belonging to the latter. The horses and donkeys were nowhere to be seen.

"What is the meaning of this?" he shouted.

The man positioned in the middle of the human line spoke without so much as moving his eyes or lowering his spear. "My name is Sir Hargit Gray. His Lordship has ordered us to follow you to the treasure, and he has given me his full permission to use force if necessary."

Sir Willam sheathed his sword and pushed through the line of dwarves so that the tip of the man's spear pressed into his chest. His breath blew heavily through his nose as he stared daringly into Sir Hargit's eyes. "That settles it, then, doesn't it?

Lord Barnum will get his treasure, so force will not be necessary. You can go home now, Sir."

Sir Hargit looked up at him, adjusting the grip on his spear without letting it fall from Sir Willam's chest. "I would beg to differ. These dwarves are outlaws. That is excuse enough to use force. And tell me, why were they leaving with Lord Barnum's treasure?"

"It is not yer treasure, ya pampered little twit!" Delvic contested.

Both sides went into a tense dance of giving and taking a single step, although none began stabbing or hacking.

"Nobody has to die today!" Sir Willam declared. "We can solve this peacefully."

"How?" asked Delvic. "I don't see no peace in this!"

"The dwarf is right," Sir Hargit said, "and the world will be a better place when this group is out of it. Stand aside, Sir, and my men will put the island to rights."

Sir Willam stared into the eyes of the man in front of him. His company of outcasts was outnumbered, backed into a corner. Now he understood that ancient carving in the tower. Now he knew what the black-bearded dwarf had meant when he said "your kind." This was not about treasure, and this was not about him or Yevnir.

"Do not pretend you followed me for the treasure. Please. If you are going to kill a man, at least give him a reason that is true."

"There is no need for you to die, Sir."

"There is no need for anyone to die!" He felt the rage behind his eyes, felt his hand twitch as it yearned for his sword.

Sir Hargit tightened his grip, narrowed his eyes, and shouted, "Forward!" Sir Willam smacked Sir Hargit's spear tip away and yanked his own sword from its scabbard. The dwarves and their dogs clashed with Lord Barnum's men, dodging, ducking, and parrying thrusts.

Sir Willam leveled his sword to Sir Hargit, initiating their dance. Behind them, the couple joined in the fight, picking up and throwing volleys of rocks over the dwarves' heads.

Miss Borteau's eyes rolled back in her head as she began to chant some horrific spell. The trees shook violently, the mountain itself crying from its depths. Sir Willam took a step back and turned his head to the side without taking his eyes off his adversary.

"Protect her!" he shouted, and the couple rushed to her side.

Hargit thrust his spear and Willam dodged it, returning with a lateral slash that barely missed his neck. "You can't win this!" said Hargit. "There are more of us coming!"

Willam slashed again in response, this time sending a spark off Hargit's chest plate. Then he was hit with the hard wood of a spear butt. He stumbled back, but before he could steady his feet to strike again, a loud crack sounded from the wood line. Wood splitting, splintering, and then . . . *crash!*

A guttural scream flew from the mouth of one of Lord Barnum's men.

Sir Willam glanced to his left to follow the screams. The top half of a tree had fallen on one of the green-cloaked men, crushing his legs. Another thundering crack. The witch's chant grew louder, more sinister. A spear tip grazed his cheek as he ducked away from it. His opponent was panicking now, looking from one side of his lines to the other as they fought. The sound of another crash sent him over the edge. Sir Hargit lunged.

Willam spun away from the attack and stopped with his body square to his opponent in time to see two explosions of dirt from behind Sir Hargit's line. Dirt rained down on them all in clumps, and the severed hands of his own men smacked against Hargit's helm as they fell. The green-cloaked knight looked down at the hands with an expression of pure revulsion then passed Sir Willam's shoulder to Miss Borteau, who had caused the explosions with her magic. "Some knight you are, Sir Willam," he said, spitting on the ground between them. "You fight alongside these monsters? This witch? How could you swear your vows on the Sydia when the book tells us to be rid of such creatures? You are no knight!"

The two clashed. Their blades caught at the crossguards, and Sir Willam made a swooping motion with his leg to trip Sir Hargit to the ground. Barnum's knight fell hard. Sir Willam stood over him for a split second and started to swing his sword in a downward motion, when another green-cloaked soldier met him with a spear thrust that he barely parried.

The Edran knight swung a wide stroke to create distance, and before he could close it, a gray dog tackled the green cloak and viciously ripped at his throat. The man screamed and flailed as Sir Willam looked back at Sir Hargit. He was past Sir Willam now, behind the line of Brochmail Brothers, which was slowly losing ground. Hargit was on his back, scooting toward the witch and the multi-armed couple, fumbling to unsheathe his sword after losing his spear.

Walking him down, Willam prayed to gods he didn't even believe in. "Oros, Silas, Ebry, let the violence stop with this one death." His hopes were shattered when he saw the man's eyes widen then his lips part into a victorious smile.

"The witch!" Hargit shouted. "Aim for the witch!"

Another two trees cracked loudly behind him, more screams followed, and the knight turned to see the fight. The line of Arduny men had broken. Delvic screamed some unintelligible phrase of encouragement through the sound of splitting trees and screaming men, raising his sword above his head before the charge.

"Take the shot!" yelled Sir Hargit.

Sir Willam frowned and squinted at first, then his eyes went wide, and he rushed toward Miss Borteau as he recognized the oncoming wave through the chaos. A dozen more cloaks of green. An arrow whizzed past his face. Time seemed to slow as his eyes followed its trajectory. "No!"

The arrow lodged itself at the base of her throat—the same throat he had wanted to wring with his own hands moments ago. All the youth drained from her face immediately. She was that hunched old lady in her gravelly hut once more, withered and wasting away. Blood trickled from her lips and shot out in droplets when she spit, choking, clawing at the arrow shaft.

Their eyes met. She was shocked, incredulous, her eyes like a child's. He wanted to say he was sorry right then and there. He tried to communicate it with his eyes. It was too late. Miss Borteau fell face-first to the ground, forcing the arrow farther through her throat. Her blond hair already started to soak up the blood that puddled beneath her.

The couple rushed to her aid, as if there were a thing they could do. The mountain went silent, and the trees held straight, but the fighting went on.

Hargit leaped to his feet and took a swing at Sir Willam. He caught it with his blade and stepped backward as he blocked another, steel clashing with loud twangs. Dodging another blow, Willam threw out his gloved fist and caught Hargit square on the nose, sending him back a few steps toward the cave. From behind him came a guttural scream, fast approaching. He turned to parry the attack, swinging his sword blindly and connecting with steel. Then grabbing this new attacker's sword arm, he head-butted him with all his might. His own forehead cracked on impact, opening with a steady trickle of blood like a leak in a vase.

The move was enough to disorient his attacker. Before the green cloak could reorient, the dark steel of Sir Willam's new blade was being forced into the base of his throat, that sweet spot above the chest plate, the same spot Miss Borteau had taken an arrow.

Willam gritted his teeth spitefully, pushed his blade slowly, and took the time to look into the eyes of the man he was killing, even with Hargit charging him from behind. The truth was the eyes he saw did not give him the satisfaction he was expecting. They were the same incredulous child's eyes he had seen on Miss Borteau. The green cloak had light-brown hair and a pudgy, freckled face, ruined by terror. He couldn't have been older than four and ten.

He thought of Tren, the young spotter whom he had failed to save from the sirens on the *Loyal Blue*. He thought of his little brother Sampson. He thought of his promise that nobody was going to die.

The boy's body fell limp to the ground. Sir Willam's dark blade slid from his young throat straight into the next attack.

Hargit blocked the first swing, but the spiked hilt of Sir Willam's sword crashed violently into his cheek on the back swing, opening his face in a spraying burst of blood and saliva. It was as he fell that Sir Willam reassessed the battle. Four dwarves had fallen, including the black-bearded dwarf and one graybeard. Figurt had taken an arrow to his shoulder, and Barasina had a large gash on one cheek and along one of her arms. The dogs had scattered the fighting, ferociously tearing apart their enemies. Still, many of them were falling, and another dozen green-cloaked men had shown up from the woods, some of them archers picking away at any dwarf or dog singled out from the fight.

"Tighten your ranks!" Willam shouted. "Fall back to the cave!" Once they were in there, they'd be trapped, he knew, but at least it would give them a second to organize. Delvic was the first to fall back, shouting to Sir Willam as he passed.

"We can't hold 'em fer long! You'd better have a plan!"

His bald head was spattered with blood and his short sword was dripping. The knight ducked an arrow and then struck down another attacker. The couple were in the cave now, and the dwarves were in full retreat. Barnum's men seemed hesitant to follow.

Sir Willam was the last one to push his way through the vines, arrows barely missing his head. He looked back before the darkness.

Straight ahead, stepping over bodies and around fallen trees was a suit of shining steel armor, a thick reddish-orange beard, and a look of pure malice.

CHAPTER THIRTEEN

"Lord Barnum is out there." The magic trick Miss Borteau had done to light up the treasure trove had died with her, so what was left of the company huddled around the knight in the darkness of the cave, sheltered by a heaping pile of gold bars and coins. "Delvic, how many bows have you?"

Delvic sparked a flint to a torch as a few others did the same. With the little bit of light, the dwarf leader took count of his brothers.

"Three," he said, but an orange-bearded dwarf next to him shook his head.

"Brim fell out there. We're only two now."

"Right, it's two, then," Delvic looked from the dwarf back to Sir Willam, his jaw clenched. "We have to run fer it, no other option."

"No. You won't break through the line. There's too many of them. Even with the dogs' speed, you'd be going uphill. They have the advantage." Sir Willam pointed to the light slope that led to the cave's only exit. Cracks of light peeked through the vines enough to illuminate their pitiful path of escape. The remaining dogs huffed and snarled at the entrance but stayed next to their owners.

"What do you suggest, then?" asked a dwarf Sir Willam couldn't see.

The knight wasn't ready to answer that question. Experienced in battle, yes, in bad situations, perhaps more than anyone, but he was no great strategist. He'd made a living off dumb luck, as far as he was concerned. Plans had always been a rough outline for every situation—changeable, of little consequence. If he found himself in a spot where he needed to stop and think, it was usually only to save his own life, so whatever thinking he'd done in dire times was done with levity, until this moment where he felt the burden of other lives in his hands—on his shoulders—crushing him as if the ceiling of the cave had given way and he was being asked to hold up the weight of the mountain.

Before he could answer, a deep bellowing voice came from outside of the cave. It was Lord Barnum. "Come out, Sir Willam, or we will come in!"

First clearing his throat, he shouted, "That would be a mistake, my lord." He said it with confidence, trying to sell his bluff. The dwarves and the couple looked at him cautiously, shifting where they stood, sweat and blood mixing on their brows and on their cheeks like paint on a palette.

"Have you forgotten I have your friend?" Barnum's voice seemed to slip through the vines, bounce off the moist cave walls, and attack the huddled group like a cold gust of wind.

Sir Willam had no answer for this. *Why is he here?* He paced in the dim light, coins spreading and piling beneath his feet. Barasina looked at him with wide, pleading eyes. Figurt, on the ground next to her, yanked the arrow from his shoulder with two hands, screaming and cursing from the pain.

"Then I will remind you!" shouted Lord Barnum. "Speak,

thief!" Even from this deep in the cave, the group could hear the thud of Yevnir's knees being forced to the ground.

"Will . . . leave the treasure. He . . . he will let you live. I'm sorry!" A loud cracking sound flew through the vines and echoed faintly throughout the cave.

"Yev!" Sir Willam started to run, but the dwarves got in his way. Delvic grabbed his leg, and another dwarf had him by the arm. "Let me go!"

"They'll kill you," Delvic said through gritted teeth. "They'll kill *us*." His head was snug against Willam's thigh and his arms were wrapped so tightly they were cutting off circulation. Barasina had crouched down to aid her husband, and when she looked back at the knight, he saw her eyes filled with panic and desperation.

"Alright!" Willam put his hands in the air to show he had given up. The dwarves slowly let him go, watching him carefully. Figurt had a glove in his mouth, and he was holding two of his wife's three hands so tightly that his knuckles had gone completely white.

"Ah, ahh," he groaned.

Delvic frowned at him then looked up at Sir Willam. "I'm truly sorry 'bout yer friend, but it's too late fer 'em. We must save ourselves."

Sir Willam sat on the nearest chest, his hands covering his face. He felt a tickle on his back then a furry tail against his neck. The squin nestled against him affectionately, making little squeaking noises then soft, high-pitched purrs. "How I wish Yev had never found you," he whispered. "You are too sweet and powerful for men to know."

"What will it be, knight?" the dwarf persisted.

He took in his company of dwarven comrades. Several of them were injured, panting, sweating. Each man looked toward the cave entrance, to the lines of light peeking through the vines, with an intense acceptance. They were ready to face their fate with one last burst of violence. Delvic tended to the leg of a graybeard, using a torn-off portion of his sleeve to tie the wound.

Sir Willam shook his head, thinking he could not let these brave souls die on his account, freaks or not, criminals or not. "I will come out!" he shouted. "If you promise me no harm will come to my companions."

"No," Delvic turned to him with a scowl. "Do ya really think that'll work?"

"As you wish!" shouted Lord Barnum from outside the cave.

Taking the squin gently in his hand, he set her on a pile of coins by his feet.

"Thank you all," he said, "but this treasure is not worth your lives." He stood, and to his surprise nobody stopped him as he made his way to the vines. Before stepping through them, he looked back and caught Delvic's gaze. The dwarf was shaking his head, the left side of his face illuminated by torch fire. Blood glistened on his cheek in spots and trickled from the cut above his eye. He turned back toward the vines, and taking a deep breath, he stepped into the light.

Barnum's men were positioned in full force, at least fifty strong now. Their green cloaks and fine steel armor had already become a sight he despised, but they were nothing compared to the orange beard and grinning face of their lord. Barnum stood over Yevnir, who was a few steps away from the now deceased Miss Borteau. He held the back of his head as if he could shield it from the next blow, all while groaning in agony. The crack he'd been dealt had split the skin, and lines of dark-red blood seeped through the gaps of his fingers.

"You've made the right choice, knight. Now I will take everything—the diamonds, the gold, the rubies. By Silas, I'll take the cave and find some use for it! But all of these creatures will live another day, even if it is only the one."

All he could do was look around at them—the bodies of the

dwarves, the dogs, and the witch whom he had led to this fate. Miss Borteau was on her side, her eyes still slightly open, and her mouth and neck lost to a fresh coat of crimson that dripped and pooled beside her. *No treasure in the world is worth this*, he thought. *These lives have ended because of me, because of you.* He glared at his friend, wriggling in the dirt and blood of his own failed plans.

"Why?" Sir Willam said through gritted teeth.

Lord Barnum raised his hands and smirked. "Because I am a merciful man."

"No. Why did you come here? We were going to bring you back your gold."

"Were you?"

"He's lying, my lord!" shouted one of the green cloaks. "The dwarves were making off with it."

Lord Barnum smiled. "You see, Sir Willam? It has been my experience that you cannot trust Edrans. They are dishonest, much like dwarves. When you are dishonest, when you steal, there are consequences. That is behind us though. Now you will call the squin to you, and you will hand it over to me."

"Her," Sir Willam corrected.

"Yes, you'll hand *her* over to me."

"There is enough treasure in that cave to buy the continent. You want the squin to find you more?"

The lord put his foot on Yevnir's back and forced it down flat. "I have been taking notes from your friend, it seems. Greed is a funny thing. Contagious."

"And if I refuse?"

Now Lord Barnum smiled from ear to ear. He had seemed to abandon what few lordly mannerisms or noble facades he had presented in his castle. He was in the wild now, an animal without remorse. Sir Willam couldn't help but imagine fighting him one on one. The lord was a big, broad-shouldered, and clearly ruthless man, but the knight had known men like this, and every time he faced them alone he had killed them without fail.

Barnum was a picture of amusement when he said, "Then I will kill this wretch, and I will make you watch as I kill every single monster in that cave. One by one. Until you're so riddled with guilt that you take your own life as soon as I give you the chance. You're that kind of man. I can see it. Feeling pity for these creatures. Besides, if she is in that cave, I will find her anyway."

"Do it," cried Yevnir. "Give him what he wants!"

Sir Willam gritted his teeth. He had no choice. "Squin! Come here!" he shouted. It had never worked like that before. The little creature had made it quite clear she would not be summoned at will. She came and went when she was needed, but only if she wanted to be of use.

"What's happening out there?" Delvic shouted from within the cave.

"Don't worry, Delvic. Everything is under control." Turning toward the vines, Lord Barnum and all his men now behind him, the knight watched for the squin's approach. He doubted she would come.

They waited in near silence for the squin. There were no sounds besides the light rustling of leaves, the faint groans of Yevnir, and the distant and sporadic cries of Figurt as he battled his wound.

"Call for her again," the lord demanded.

Sir Willam turned to face him, if only to say it would not work. He held his tongue though, noticing something peculiar behind the rows of men. They looked like branches jutting out from the ground, and his first thought was they were part of one of the trees the witch felled during the battle. Only, when he studied them closer, they were moving, bouncing slowly as if they were jumping—no, trotting. They were not branches. They were antlers. As they came closer, Willam recognized the features—cobwebs and moss, a crown of twenty points. It was the elk.

"There she is!" Lord Barnum exclaimed.

Turning abruptly, the knight watched the squin sheepishly walk out from beneath the vines. The tiniest thing. She sauntered her little orange-and-black-striped body forward as if she were in trouble. Everybody watched with such intensity. Her head was down, and she whimpered the softest cries. Yevnir raised his head and grunted something unintelligible. The knight was the only one who was not enthralled by her presence.

The elk, thought Sir Willam. *What was it doing?* He turned again as the elk changed course. It was coming straight for them now. But even odder, its footsteps were deafening. Thunderous. They all felt them.

Barnum and his men wheeled around curiously toward the noise, forgetting the squin entirely to deal with what they must've thought was some sort of small earthquake. Trees seemed to be dropping in the forest behind the elk as it charged toward them.

"What in Oros's name?" Lord Barnum cursed. "Shoot the beast!"

Sir Willam squinted, stood on the tips of his toes, and stepped up on a rock to see over the line, until finally he saw it. The trees were not falling because of some remnant magic but rather because of a giant pair of legs. Barnum's men were too caught up with the charging elk to see what approached them.

"Shoot the damned thing!" Barnum screamed.

From his peripheral vision, the knight barely registered one more oddity. Yevnir was gone. He was no longer under Lord Barnum's boot, lying in the dirt, nor was he anywhere to be found. Willam thought to himself with equal parts disdain and relief, *I guess I cannot blame an opportunist for taking an opportunity.*

The first arrow whistled through the air and clattered off the elk's antlers, taking bits of moss and cobweb with it. The elk was coming at full speed now, leaping gracefully through the underbrush. A few more shots stuck into trees around it or sailed past its sleek body. It was moving so quickly that Barnum's men could not place their shots. But that wouldn't last for long.

"Give me that!" Lord Barnum yanked a longbow from one of his men. "Your father never took you hunting, did he?" The soldier could do nothing but step back and take his lord's insult. The footsteps were getting louder now, shaking the earth. Pebbles by the mountain base trembled in their wake. By the time Barnum's men saw it, they were too late. The elk darted to the side as another volley of arrows missed its hide. "Where is it going?" the lord shouted.

Sir Willam's eyes grew wide. He stumbled backward then fell to the ground as two trees came hurtling high overhead, crashing into the mountain and careening down until other trees caught them.

"Silas save me," he said, once again begging protection from gods he didn't believe in.

Barreling through the wood line, a towering figure roared its horrifying battle cry. Everybody put their hands to their ears as they looked up at the figure bursting through the trees.

He was covered from neck to knee in light-brown cloth, enough to carpet half the city of Biverna. There were stains of moss and vines growing from various seams in the fabric and weaving through his long black hair. His beard was so thick there were whole families of birds and squirrels living in it, fleeing in waves from the action, and his eyes were like blue stained-glass windows, with bags under them the size of the hammocks on Tessara's ship. The giant raised his arms and bared his teeth to the armored men.

"Arokis," muttered the knight.

Lord Barnum gathered himself from the same petrified state as the rest of them and shouted, "Kill him!"

Arokis moved first, swiping a line of men off their feet and kicking two archers into the spears of their own comrades. Suddenly, Sir Willam noticed a small group had broken off and was coming for him. He struggled to get to his feet. Backing up slowly toward the cave, he unsheathed his sword, eyeing the four men approaching with their spears leveled at his chest. They were trapping him, forcing him back into the cave.

From behind him came the jarring sound of Yevnir's voice. "Charge!"

Yevnir came sprinting through the vines chucking gold bars with all his might. The dwarves on their dogs vaulted past him, taking the spearmen off guard and trampling through them with ease.

"Come on, then, Will!" shouted Yevnir. "Don't let us fight alone!" Sir Willam smirked as he joined the fray, rushing at the men of Arduny, kicking and slashing wildly as they collided.

Lord Barnum's men were so shocked by the giant stomping through their lines that they couldn't organize to face the dwarves. They scattered, and each man fought alone. The dwarves fought even more ferociously than before, stepping around their dead brothers to get to the enemy. Sir Willam heard *shink* as his sword penetrated chainmail and crashed through the ribs of his opponent. As that man fell, another ran to take his place, but when the two squared to engage each other, Arokis's giant hand plucked the enemy off his feet. His green robe shot over his head as Arokis flipped him then sent him soaring behind his shoulder and over the treetops.

The knight looked up in awe at the towering figure. A volley of arrows stuck into the giant's arm and Arokis roared, turning violently.

Lord Barnum only needed to see the anger in the giant's eyes to drop his bow.

"Retreat!" he yelled. Flickers of orange were all Sir Willam saw of the lord as he went into an all-out sprint, passing his own men then weaving between dead bodies and fallen trees. Arokis kicked a few more men near him then stopped to let them retreat. They scattered into the woods and went fumbling to safety with their green cloaks flailing behind them.

"Do ya see that, brothers?" Delvic raised his sword in victory. "Arduny men are running from us fer a change!" The dwarves cheered thunderously. Sir Willam felt wrong to be doing it with all these bodies at his feet, but the moment overtook him, and he cheered along with them, pumping his sword over his head and shouting.

...

Soon they were all alone at the mouth of the cave. Barasina and Figurt came out gingerly from beneath the vines, their wounds wrapped in bloodied cloth. Sir Willam was talking to Delvic as the other dwarves loaded their brothers grimly onto the backs of their great beasts. "I can't begin to tell you how sorry I am for bringing you into this. I didn't know they would follow us. I swear it."

"I know ya didn't. I don't blame you." Delvic turned his head to where Yevnir stood, talking to a crouched Arokis. The height difference between them, even with Arokis crouching, made the difference between Sir Willam and Delvic's height seem insignificant. "Do you think this was all part of his plan?" Delvic asked, still looking at Yevnir and the giant. "The squin, the giant, 'nd all the rest?"

"I don't believe he could foresee all of this, although he will claim he did."

Delvic shook his head. "I'll not let 'em leave with the treasure. Ya know that, right?"

"You have your gold now. I don't know what you did before,

or who you did it too, but you don't need to anymore. I can be sure of that. So, what will the brothers do next?"

Watching his brothers tend to the dead, Delvic answered, "What we've always done, Sir Willam—survive."

The two shook hands and the knight parted toward Figurt and Barasina. "Will you be alright, Figurt?"

"I have three other hands to use while my shoulder heals," he said cheerfully, although wincing, "and a wife who'll take great care of me. It hurts, but I'll be fine."

"I'm sorry . . . about Miss Borteau, and the things I said in there."

Barasina frowned and shook her head, two of her hands steadying her husband. "It's alright, Sir Willam. Without you, we never would have spoken to her. I wish we could have had a friend, someone like us." She stifled tears and the knight put a hand on her shoulder.

"You will have a child, and the dwarves will see you differently now. I know they will. I wish you both the best." The two of them walked by and Sir Willam went toward Yevnir and the giant. The squin came scurrying out of whatever hole she had been hiding in and climbed up his leg until she was perched upon his shoulder.

"She likes you better than she ever liked me," Yevnir said, smiling.

"Are you going to introduce me to Arokis?"

The giant reached out his hand, and Sir Willam grasped the tip of his pointer finger and shook, although the hand didn't move. "Yevnir has told me a lot about you, Sir," Arokis said. "You are unlike other men." His voice was deep, but he was no longer the terrifying brute he had been in battle. He had settled into a kind and warm demeanor. Sir Willam had a feeling this was his true self.

The knight smiled and let go of the giant's fingertip. "I thank you, Arokis, for your kindness and for your help. I believe Yevnir underestimated the power of your friendship. He was under the impression you would kill us all if you saw us with Lord Barnum's men."

Yevnir shot Willam a look like he had been betrayed.

"Oh, I would have," Arokis said with a chuckle, "without any doubt. The old elk told me what was what though. She told me you were different from the knights of old. She told me you stopped your companion from killing her at her drinking pool."

The knight remembered seeing the elk for the first time on the mountainside, and how he had stayed Varro's hand from killing the creature. He thanked the Druid silently for his luck, and unlike his prayers to Silas and all the other Sydian gods, he meant this thanks from the bottom of his heart.

"And the dwarves?" asked Sir Willam. "Would you have spared them?"

"It is not easy for a giant to distinguish dwarves from men, I'm afraid, but I have no qualms with the dwarves. Lord Barnum and his ancestors have killed dwarves and giants alike. We share in that pain."

Yevnir nodded. "Arokis was telling me it was time something be done about the—"

"Epulites," Sir Willam interrupted. "Lord Barnum is an Epulite."

Arokis flinched. "The Epulites were gone long ago, Sir. They pushed us into the forests and the mountains until a great wizard stood to defend us, and when they retreated to do the same to other creatures, in other lands, the wizard followed them. No, the Barnums are not Epulites. They are merely evil men who took up the mantle of the killers who came before."

"The Epulites were the servants of the goddess Ebry," Yevnir added. "She thought humans would have to fight the other races to stay alive, and so to save them from a gruesome war, she made the Epulites. In the Sydia, they went to the continent after Pastora, and did the same thing to the creatures there, until the wizard showed them the truth and convinced them to stop fighting for Ebry. That's why he's called the Forgiver in the Sydia. Some people even think Ebry sent the wizard herself, to fix her mistake, although it was too late. See . . . it's all real, Will. Pastora is proof."

Sir Willam turned around to see that half of the dwarves were getting ready to ride away with their dead, while the others stood guard at the entrance to the cave. Figurt and Barasina were wrapping Miss Borteau in a cloth with their many hands. Barasina cried silently as she worked, tears dripping onto the dead witch's wrappings, and as she finished, she took the vial she'd been given from her pocket and kissed it.

"And where are the Epulites now?" he asked. "How could they leave without fixing what they broke here? How could they not come back when the Forgiver showed them they were wrong?"

"Oh, those Epulites are long dead by now," said Arokis. "They live to the age of normal men. I do believe they come back from time to time—the descendants, I mean—but perhaps their ancestors never told them what happened here. Maybe they forgot on purpose so they could move on."

"Well, I do not forget," Sir Willam said sternly, "and I do not move on until my job is done. I will stay here, and together we will fight."

Yevnir looked at Willam pleadingly, but it was Arokis who spoke. "You came to rescue the Goldleaf, and that you have done. Your journey here is at an end, Sir Willam. This is our island, our fight, and we must fight it alone."

"You don't need to," Sir Willam argued. "I can help." Yevnir put his hand on Willam's shoulder, and they made eye contact for a moment. *Do not take me from this fight you've brought me into*, thought the knight. Yevnir did not say anything though and walked away to help the dwarves. Sir Willam was left alone with Arokis, staring up into his giant eyes from so far below them. "Let me help you, Arokis. There is no need to fight them alone." His heart yearned for Horntree, but his conscience could not let this injustice go. He'd sworn a vow after all, and it had once meant everything to him.

The giant smiled warmly. "Pastora is my home," he said. "When I was young, my mother would walk with me from one side of the island to the other, just to show me that we were free to walk. That was the time between the Epulites and the Barnums—a time of peace." He sighed deeply, looking up at the green mountain. A breeze swayed the pines. "Those years were so few I barely remember them now. But I know they existed. They are there, in my memory, somewhere out of reach, and you have reminded me that I will never find them."

The giant chuckled softly, looking back down at Sir Willam. "I always thought, if I tried hard enough, I could remember those days, when I could walk across the island in broad daylight without having to fight for my place here. I do have to fight though. You've shown me that today, and for that I thank you. This is my land, and these are my people." The giant looked sorrowfully at the bodies scattered on the ground. "They need me. I see that now, and so too do your people need you. There are peoples of all races in Edra who have been forced to hide as we have. Yevnir has told me of their existence, though he seems to think they have gone extinct. They have not. I know they have not. They are hiding in the mountains and in the glens, in the forests and in the deepest caves. Fight for *them*, Sir Willam, or nobody else will."

Sir Willam remembered the few creatures he had fought in Edra—the Sceuorg, the Serpetia, the Blavel. These beings he had considered monsters. Which of them had been protecting themselves before he was called upon to kill them? Which had he killed before attempting diplomacy?

Lastly, he thought about the poor old woman whom he'd watched burn at the stake, the first of the two witches whose deaths he'd been responsible for. He turned his head to see Miss Borteau, lying there lifeless. *I am no better than Lord Barnum*, he thought. *The Epulites' mission has lived on through me as it has through him. That ends today.*

He felt a fire behind his eyes, a palpable yearning to do better, to *be* better. He drew his sword and put the point into the dirt. With his gloved hands resting on the hilt, he knelt before the giant and looked to the ground. Shame and determination mingled within him, along with something else entirely unfamiliar—faith. Not faith in the gods of the Sydia, the deities that in Edra were denounced almost exclusively in the village he grew up in. No, it was faith in something more powerful than gods, more potent than religious devotion—it was faith in purpose.

"I will fight for them, Arokis," Sir Willam said. "On my honor, I will fight for them until my last breath."

CHAPTER FOURTEEN

The Next Morning

The knight pushed his linens off him. The sun peered into the room through a four-paned window, and he could see the tops of Bivernian buildings from his bed. Their flat plains of grass and flower gardens seemed to be in full bloom after the days of rain. He may have taken a moment to admire the beauty of Biverna if he weren't in so much pain. His arms ached from yesterday's battle. It hurt even to yawn from the hit he had taken on his nose, and the small gash on his face from Sir Hargit's spear felt like it was going to reopen.

After the battle, Arokis had spoken to the dwarves about the war to come. Sir Willam stayed to listen then took his leave of them with some sadness, shaking each man's hand tenderly and saying sorry for this chaos that was, at least in his mind, of his own making.

After a short walk, he and Yevnir had found the two horses and the two donkeys following the path back through the forest. That night, they had rented rooms in the Hollow Mountain Inn, using what little gold Delvic allowed them to take from the cave.

As he sat up on the edge of the bed, he reflected on it all. He had been in Pastora less than a week, and in that time he had tricked pirates; employed dwarves, a witch, and a multiarmed couple; fought a lord; followed a squin to treasure; and shaken hands with a giant. Yevnir couldn't have planned for all of it, and if he had, he wouldn't have ended up poorer than he started.

There was something in Sir Willam's mind he could not make sense of.

In fact, it was sitting right in front of him, leaning against the wall. Attun, the sword he had found in the cave, was in his old scabbard still; its wood handle and tree-shaped silver pommel stuck out from the black leather sheath. It hid out of reach of the sunlight coming in through the window, tucked into the corner as it had been tucked into the deepest part of that treasure-filled cave.

"Attun," he said.

Yevnir had gathered all of the treasure with the squin's help, and he had given it all, including the Ahkovan pirates' loot, to Arokis, who put it in that cave at the base of the Hollow Mountain. Had he known about the sword though? He couldn't have. His not knowing the location of the treasure was pivotal to the plan. Besides, if he had ever found that chest, the lock would have already been broken. Yevnir was not the type to leave a chest unopened.

There was something odder still. The words "Nagri Attun" engraved in the blade were the same words his priests had taught him as a child. Not Sydian priests, who were much greater in number, but the priests of his own religion, if it was a religion at all. He had never met anyone outside of his village who knew the words or knew of his beliefs. He had scarcely met a person outside of his village who even knew the village existed.

Sir Willam grew up in a quiet, secluded place, where they kept to their own ways and held their own beliefs. "Nagri Attun" was a phrase the priests in his village would use in their teachings. It meant something like "nature's grace." Willam rubbed the sleep from his eyes and thought, *By the Druid, how could those words end up in a Pastoran cave?*

He stood up, painfully and groggily, then snatched the sword from the corner. A loud knock came from his door. "You up yet, Will?" came Yevnir's voice.

"I'm awake. Give me a moment to get dressed."

Yevnir ignored this request and came barging in, looking anxious. He had changed into a fresh wine-colored tunic and combed his hair out. His eyes and cheeks were still slightly swollen from the Ahkovan pirates' torture, and his lip had a slight cut still from where it had been split.

"What's wrong with you? I'm getting dressed," Sir Willam looped his belt through his scabbard and wrapped his cloak around his shoulders.

"Our ship's ready," said Yevnir, "but I've just gotten word from Arokis. Barnum's men were spotted coming down the river. They'll be here within a few hours. We need to go."

The knight pinned his bronze brooch to his cloak and picked up his heavy saddle bag from the floor. "Right," he said, "come on, squin. It's time to leave."

The little creature was curled up in a ball atop a pillow on the far side of the room. She purred gently and looked up at the two of them with her wild yellow eyes then sauntered toward Sir Willam and climbed up his leg and torso until she was on his shoulder. Together, the three of them hurried down the stairs to the area where the knight had first met Tessara and her brother, Varro. It was almost empty, besides the barkeep sweeping and a server taking chairs off tables, and in the booth where Sir Willam had first talked to Captain Tessara, a hooded man sat drinking a cup of ale.

Yevnir rushed out the door and Sir Willam followed behind him, but before he had left the inn, the hooded man shouted, "Knight!"

He stopped where he was, one hand on the door. Yevnir looked back at him inquisitively. "Go on," he said. "I'll meet you at the docks." Yevnir nodded to him, and Sir Willam turned back into the inn, letting the wood door creak closed behind him. He walked over to the table, the squin still resting on his shoulder. He set down his saddle bag and took off his sword belt to sit.

"Varro," he said. "I recognized your voice. Have you come for revenge?"

The pirate took his hood off, revealing his crooked and bruised nose from when Sir Willam had hit him with his sword pommel. His eyes were slightly bloodshot, and his face was full of anger. "They are . . . She is . . . dead?" He spoke slowly, with effort, his voice infused with his thick Ahkovan accent.

The knight remembered how he had threatened to kill the whole crew up in the mountain after he and Varro fought. *He has gone these days thinking his sister and all of their crew were killed*, he thought. *It must've taken him a whole day to row from the Sivkara to the shore, then limp all the way to Biverna*. He felt terrible, even though the pirates had taken him hostage and beaten his friend near to death. Varro was a brother before he was a pirate, and he probably felt like he had failed to protect his sister. Sir Willam thought of how he had failed Tren. He imagined how he would have felt if it was truly Sampson he had failed.

"She is not dead," Sir Willam said, not a knight to a pirate, but an elder brother to another elder brother. "Your sister and the rest of the crew are in Lord Barnum's dungeon. Well . . . save a few, who are, indeed, dead."

Varro closed his eyes and nodded, and for a long moment they sat there in silence, until Sir Willam had the urge to fix what he had broken. "When I leave, ask the barkeep to point you in the direction of Figurt and Barasina's house. They will have information for you that may lead to a way to get your sister back. I cannot tell you more, just that something is coming, and you might be able to save her if you are a part of it. But, Varro . . ."

"Hm?"

"You will have to fight, and your comrades will be . . . well, different from the crew you are used to." Sir Willam donned a slight smirk, stood, gathered his things, and patted Varro's shoulder before leaving the inn.

Outside, a group of kids shouted and laughed as they kicked a brown leather ball between two sticks in the dirt street. Market stands were being re-erected all throughout Biverna. Foreign goods and local produce were brought out in crates to be displayed. An orange-bearded dwarf rode proudly past him on his gray dog, giving Sir Willam a nod.

"Woohoo!" a child's voice rang through the bustling streets. Ardee ran in a celebratory circle, his teammates cheering him on. When the boy saw Sir Willam, his eyes lit up and his smile grew even wider. "Sir Willam! Everyone, it's the knight. I told you he was real!" The young Simerian ran to Sir Willam and hugged his leg.

The knight laughed and tousled the boy's hair. "Way to go, Ardee," he said. "They are letting you play now?"

"Yes, and I am good!"

"I see that! How did you change their minds?"

"I told them my family name, and they all knew it."

"So you chose one, then?"

"Yes!"

"Go on. What is it?"

The young boy backed away and looked at Sir Willam with the cheekiest grin. "Hornsby."

The knight was shocked. "Uh . . . that's . . . that's a good name, if I do say so myself." He hadn't thought much about passing his name on to someone else, but when he had, he always imagined it would be a child of his own. Ardee clearly was not that, but then again, he was nobody's child. He was an orphan, as Sir Willam was. Why shouldn't he share his name?

"How did my name change their minds?" he asked.

Before he could get an answer, he was being swarmed by the children, who shouted, "Sir Willam Hornsby! Sir Willam Hornsby! The liberator of Dunford Abbey, slayer of the Sceuorg!" Apparently, these were the only two of his many titles that had made it this far west.

He laughed at their praise and shook their hands and gave out hugs, and they coddled the squin as if she were his pet, until their interest in him had drained and they went back to playing their ball game. It was just Ardee left standing next to Sir Willam.

The young Simerian looked up at him with wide, hopeful eyes, and said, "Will you take me with you, Sir? Back to Edra? I could be your squire."

"Ah, no, Ardee. I'm afraid not. My adventures are too dangerous for a young boy, even a little warrior like yourself."

"Please, could I . . ." Ardee saw he would not be able to convince the knight and instead asked, "Where did you find that orange squirrel?"

Sir Willam chuckled, peering down at the squin, who rested on his shoulder. "She came to *me*. She's a squin, a very magical creature."

"Wow," Ardee said, "that is amazing."

The way the child looked at the squin was the same way he imagined Yevnir must've looked at that treasure when he'd found it. Suddenly, Sir Willam had an idea. He cupped the squin in his palms and lowered her by his belly.

"I'll tell you what," he said. "Will you look after her for me?" And he put her gently into Ardee's small hands. Then he pulled the last Pastoran coin he had from his coin purse and held it up by his face, kneeling to Ardee's eye level. "Give this to her later today, and she will take you to a very special man. His name is Arokis." He gestured for Ardee to come closer and whispered, "He is a *giant!*"

Ardee's mouth hung wide open, and he cradled the squin in his arms as if she were the most fragile baby ever born. "A giant?" he whispered.

"Yes. But more importantly, he is a good man. Find him. Tell him the name you chose and that you came to make it stand for something better. He will know what that means. And when you are old enough, come find me. I will make a knight of you then."

He smiled at the boy and tousled his hair one more time, then he stroked the squin's head with a finger and she squealed happily. "Do this last task for me, my friend," he said to her, "and then go back to your family. We both must, us loyal friends. I cannot thank you enough for what you have done." He leaned down and kissed her furry head then stood to leave toward the docks, nodding to Ardee and waving to the children playing their ball game.

In his room, Yevnir had told him that Lord Barnum's men would be there within hours, so naturally he took his time walking back through Biverna. He had not been there long enough to say he would miss it, nor had he had the most pleasant experiences since he first walked through this street, but nevertheless this little town and the island itself would hold a place in his heart forever.

He admired once more the beauty of the Bivernian roofs; the dark, wet-looking stone and moss of the older buildings;

and the bounty of color that filled the streets. In Edra there was a common myth that Pastora was "the land of luck." Sir Willam did not see it this way. When he remembered Pastora in the days to come, he would not think of luck, chance, or history. He would think of faith, rebellion, and restoration. He would think of Ardee, growing up with the influence of a kindhearted giant and a gritty bunch of dwarves. He would think of what creatures he had not encountered on the island and all those who had been rendered extinct.

It would remind him to be better, to protect the innocent, as he had vowed to do, even if those innocents were not human and excluding a certain very guilty friend.

As he reached the port, with its many outstretching docks, he stopped. The sun peeked over the mountain behind him, and the morning brightened drastically. Sir Willam looked back at Biverna, with all its shops and markets, and the Hollow Mountain looming in all its great greenness over the town. A flock of yellow torpins flew overhead toward the mountain, returning from their journey. He smiled then, thinking of home.

The port was in its full splendor this morning. Merchant ships rolled in with the tide, displaying the banners of their homelands, some of which Sir Willam had never seen. There looked to be at least a dozen ships on the horizon waiting for their turn to dock and sell their goods. He had not realized how large the port was when he had come into it, but from this side it somehow seemed enormous.

Among the banners displayed on the sails of the many vessels and cogs, he immediately recognized the Antaeus sigil, and it forced a smile onto his lips; it was a black giant on a light-blue background, reaching to the heavens to grasp the stars. *The* Loyal Blue, he thought, but as he moved closer, he quickly realized it was too small a cog to be the *Loyal Blue* and his smile left him.

The ship's crewmen were busy loading and unloading crates of produce and barrels of Bordaen wine and different kinds of Edran and Morridan ale. Their captain, a burly man standing near the cog, dealt with a local vendor. His beard was unkempt and the color of oak, and when he smiled, he revealed a few golden teeth. Through the bustling of the crewmen, Sir Willam saw Yevnir bent over a small trunk that he seemed to be loading onto the ship. His curly black hair and wine-colored tunic made him easily discernible from afar.

It was another sight that drew his attention though, near a different ship. A big man, rough looking with a slightly ripped and faded red shirt, was squatting down on the dock tying his ship to the moorings. It was the hands that gave him away. *Raf.* His three-fingered hands were unmistakable. Sir Willam immediately changed his course.

"Is that you, Raf?" he asked as he approached.

"Oh, well if it ain't Sir Willam 'Ornsby his own self! Glad to see you, mate." Raf quickly wrapped and tied the rest of the rope to the mooring and stood straight.

"Did you jump ship so soon? Why leave the *Loyal Blue*?"

"Aye, I quit." Raf looked over at his new ship, the crew slowly disembarking, then back at the knight. "Captain Tarrick is done with this route. He swore the *Loyal Blue* would never sail to Pastora again. That's when I left 'em. Your quest was successful, was it?"

"Yes, in many ways, I'd say, and in some others a failure. Why did you leave the old crew though? What's in Pastora for you?"

"Not in Pastora." Raf's face lit up and he pointed to the ocean. "Out there. Didn't you see them, Sir? What's more beautiful, more terrifying, more alive? The sirens are in season, and I mean to hunt 'em."

"Terrifying, I can agree with, but a necklace of ears isn't

worth your life. They are dangerous beasts, Raf. You must be careful."

"That's precisely why I 'ave to see 'em again! You may get lucky enough to see 'em again too. Just be ready when you see the storm comin' on."

"Yes, that would be my luck. Let us just be glad we are too old for their songs if we are both to see them again."

"Yer never too old, Sir, if you can understand what it is yer listenin' to."

"And you understand?"

"I aim to."

"Then I can only wish you luck, Raf. I better get going though. My quest still has one last step, I'm afraid." The two shook hands and departed, but as he walked away, Sir Willam looked back at the old seaman, wondering about sirens as he often wondered about fish, and wondering if it was for the rare beauty of the creature that he chased it, or for the killing of it. The same thing he'd wondered about himself many times when he'd frustratedly thrown back a catfish too small to eat, or when he'd taken a big bass home to cook despite knowing he disliked the taste.

From the corner of his eye, Sir Willam saw the captain running over to him as he made his way to the cog. "Oi!" said the captain, "bloody hell, it's the slayer of the Sceuorg!" He reached out to shake the knight's hand. "Captain Garent, Sir. At yer service. It is a real honor."

"Thank you, Captain," said Sir Willam, "the honor is all mine." Captain Garent nodded giddily and went back to his deal with the Pastoran vendor. Yevnir was on the cog now and smiling at Sir Willam as he sat on top of his trunk. "I've felt more famous here than I ever did in Edra."

"It's a small island. Word gets around. The first thing the captain asked me was, 'Is it true he's 'ere? Is it really true?'"

Yevnir cackled. "I'm pretty sure the vendors have been talking about you. You've caused quite a stir."

Sir Willam scratched his neck and breathed out slowly. "Well," he said, "I'm looking forward to lying low."

"Who was that man you were talking to before Garent? He looked rougher than the Brochmail Brothers."

"Oh, him?" Sir Willam looked back to where Raf had been a moment ago. He was gone, as were the rest of his new crew. "He's just an old friend."

"Ah, Silas knows you have too many of those."

...

Soon after, the cog was leaving port. Captain Garent waved to his Pastoran customers, and his crew worked tirelessly on the deck. Sir Willam Hornsby and Yevnir Goldleaf sat on the lid of Yevnir's trunk, alive and no richer than before. The wind was gentle and the sun bright.

"I wanted to apologize," Yevnir said, "for all of this."

"There's no need."

"But—"

"No," Sir Willam said firmly, "when I came to this island, I thought your greed had gotten you captured and that you would never change, that all you cared about was gold and jewels and everything else was in service of attaining them. But this grand plan of yours . . . It cost people their lives, yes, but it also started something that needed to be started. It was all you."

Yevnir rubbed the back of his neck. "I wouldn't say it was all me. In fact, I . . . Ugh. I hadn't planned for all of this. You were right. This all started with my greed. I can't take the credit."

"I know."

"What?"

"I was being sarcastic. You're a greedy bastard. I just wanted you to admit it."

"I really thought I was a genius," Yevnir chuckled, "and now I'm leaving the island with less than I came with. Completely empty-handed."

"Not completely . . ."

"How do you mean?"

Sir Willam placed his saddle bag down with a clank on the space between them on the trunk lid. Yevnir's eyes widened as the knight pulled something from it, something covered in cloth. Willam pulled the cloth off to reveal the Emerald Man.

"You sneaky . . . You're giving it to me? Why?"

"Oh, I don't need it," said the knight. "Money won't fix Edra's problems or help me do what needs to be done."

Yevnir held the Emerald Man in both hands and spun it, admiring the way the light shined through it. "And what's that? What's next for Sir Willam Hornsby?"

"I'm going to fight for the creatures of Edra and help them fight for themselves, but first, I'm going home." Sir Willam looked back at Pastora, the green mountain and the green shore. As much as he would hold it in his heart, it was not his home. He thought about the pond beyond the tall grass, and he thought about his brothers, Philip and John and Sampson. Dark clouds seemed to be gathering just beyond the mountain. Clouds that might have excited him once, and certainly would still excite Raf. But he knew they wouldn't catch him this time, at least not for a while, and he was happier for it.

"Going home? To do what?" Yevnir asked, still admiring the Emerald Man.

"Well . . ." Sir Willam said. He smiled, the kind of closed-eyed smile one made after sinking their teeth into a savory cut of meat or a sweet apple pastry, and the gentle breeze kissed at his face.

"I think I'll start by going fishing."

Reece Caven is a Creative Writing Major at the University of Iowa. Born and raised in Iowa City, Reece has served his community in the Iowa National Guard, co-founded and served as secretary of the nonprofit Neighborhood Youth United, and volunteered as a wrestling coach at Iowa City High School. Reece's work has appeared in Adelaide Literary Magazine and an undergrad publication at the University of Iowa called Cave Writing Magazine.

FIND ME AT:

Instagram: reece_57
Facebook: Reece Caven
Twitter: @ReeceACaven
TikTok: @reece.caven
www.reeceacaven.com

If you enjoyed reading The Liar & the Knight, please leave a review on Amazon! Thank you!

Printed in the USA
CPSIA information can be obtained
at www.ICGtesting.com
CBHW071916130824
13144CB00008B/14

9 798990 915305